FLASHING MOUNTAIN

by

EDWIN JOHNSON

THE CHILDREN'S PRESS
LONDON AND GLASGOW

First printed 1964

CONTENTS

CHAPTER ONE

ESCAPE TO DANGER

CHARLES "Chip" Wood stumbled into an alley behind a derelict house and doubled up breathlessly.

"What a birthday," he panted bitterly. "What a perishing fifteenth birthday."

He knew that, unless in the next few minutes he lost Christian Silverman for good, he would be caught. He just could not keep going much farther.

Silverman's voice, coming from nearby, urged the gang on and startled him into one last effort to get away. Chip braced his shoulders. He tried not to admit to himself that he was afraid. But he knew what Silverman was capable of, everyone knew it. He had seen other boys who had been worked over by Silverman and the gang and they were all too scared to talk about it, even to one another.

The alley branched off between a warehouse and a junk yard and then seemed to peter out behind a pile of scrap. It was too dark to see where he was going and a mist rolling up from the Thames made things worse. It would not help him, because the gang knew this tangle of Deptford backways by the docks like river rats. This was where they operated.

He caught sight of a feeble gas lamp and came out into a small square. It was a dead end flanked by a massive wall, which he recognised as the dock boundary.

He was trapped. The wall completely surrounded the dock area and there was no way through except for the gates, and they were guarded.

9

He looked about desperately, but there was no place to hide, the blank fronts of the store buildings lining the other three sides of the square gave no hope.

He could hear the gang shouting to one another farther back, and above them all, Silverman's unmistakable voice.

"Got him now . . . dead end. Fetch him out. Fetch him for me."

"Where, Silver? Didn't see nothing."

"Down by the wall, stupid . . ."

They were only three or four minutes behind at the most. Then Chip saw the crates piled in the shadows against the wall. It was against the regulations to put anything against the wall, but some careless warehouseman had done it. They reached about half-way to the top and offered a slim chance.

Chip did not hesitate. He scrambled up, gathered himself, and jumped. His fingers hooked over the coping as the crates collapsed under his feet. With the last ounce of his strength he heaved upwards to sit astride the wall. His laboured breath hung about him like steam in the damp air.

Beyond, the flat roof of a store stretched away into the darkness. He slid down on to the asphalt surface and crouched behind the coping, hoping that the row he had made had not attracted Silverman's attention.

It was not only the violent exercise that made him breathless. When he became excited he often felt like that, as though he would suffocate. Sometimes he worried about it, but he never told anyone. He kept it to himself, like he kept so much else to himself.

He brushed his damp, sandy hair out of his eyes and drew a deep breath. He could have kicked himself for getting into such a mess. He was usually good at avoiding trouble.

There was something mouse-like about his sharp features as he glanced suspiciously around. He was a bit on the skinny side and small for his age, and being like that as well as having to live in someone else's family, it paid to keep out of trouble. Usually he managed it so well that no one noticed he was there, but sometimes—sometimes he got angry and obstinate, and then he forgot about being careful, then he felt as if he was ten feet tall and did not give tuppence for anyone. But it never lasted and always left him like now, nervous and breathless.

Tensely he strained to catch any sign of his pursuers but the only sound to break the silence was the hooting of a tug somewhere up by the Isle of Dogs. It echoed flatly from the wharves across the water before being muffled by the fog.

He chewed his thumb nervously as he waited. Then he heard them again, thudding along the alley towards him. They halted, as he had done, under the lamp. The crates were dragged away from the wall to uncover any possible hiding-place.

"Not there, you fool," came Silverman's voice, breathless and vicious. "He's farther on somewhere. Get going."

"But Silver, we'll never find him. We've searched the whole perishing area. Pack it in. We'll get him to-morrow. We know where he lives."

The complaint was cut short by a sharp smack, followed by a cry.

"There's plenty more where that came from," snarled Silverman. "That goes for the rest of you. He burnt our hut down, didn't he? I want him, and I want him now, to-night. So get going, like I said."

There was a further scuffle and the gang moved off.

Chip waited until everything was quiet again before moving. He was shaking at the narrowness of his escape.

He could still picture Silverman's fleshy face, white in the glare of the pressure lamp, and hear the high-pitched voice: "Promising kids like you *are* my business. I can use you. There's a lot going on round the docks I'm interested in. If there's a profit, I'm interested in anything. That's my motto; anything—if the price is right. Get it?"

That was not all Chip had got. He had seen the others Silverman had his hooks in, and how they finished up; reform school, borstal, and the nick.

Silverman had not liked being told about that. He had not liked it either when Chip, struggling to get free, had kicked the lamp over. The burning oil had set Silverman's hut ablaze in seconds. They had been lucky to get out alive. The marshes had been lit up for miles.

Chip grinned faintly at the memory, in spite of his chattering teeth. The trouble was he would not dare show his face around for months. Facing up to Silverman with courage screwed up for the purpose, that was one thing; but being persecuted for it afterwards, that was the rub. Anyhow, he could not stay on the roof all night. He was soaked from falling in a ditch after crossing the railway, and cold was eating into his bones. For the moment he was safe, but he was not out of the wood yet. He reckoned the best thing would be to retrace his steps hoping that none of the gang had been left behind. With any luck he could follow the railway until he was near his aunt's house. Much good that would do him when he got there, he thought dismally. He could hear her shrill voice screaming at him when she saw the state he was in. Home sweet home! He pulled a face in the darkness, and cautiously peered over the coping.

What he saw was not promising, for the pile of crates had been knocked down and he was faced with jumping to the ground, fifteen feet if it was an inch.

He decided against it. It would have been too easy to twist, or even break, an ankle.

He would have to make his way through the docks to one of the gates, and then he would need to think of a good story if he were to get out past the special police, who were always on the lookout for anyone sneaking into the stores along the quays. But anything, even being held by the police, would be better than running into Silverman again.

Having made up his mind, he turned away from the wall and surveyed the dock area. There was not much to be seen, but over to his right the fog was reflecting lights on the waterside so that a patch of sky seemed to glow.

He could just make out the superstructure of a ship. She could not have been very big, but she towered over the dock buildings, her size exaggerated in the gloom.

He decided to make for her. If she was unloading or preparing to sail, he might lose himself in the activity and smuggle on to a lorry, which would take him through the gates undetected.

The shed he was on stretched for a long way, finishing up against a road to the water. In the other direction a brightly-lit gate stood out in the surrounding darkness.

Between the gate and the waterfront the road was in semi-darkness. "First bit of luck," he muttered to himself and groped along the gutter for a rainwater pipe or stanchion to clamber down.

Just as he found a likely place he heard footsteps approaching from the direction of the gate, and dropped flat on the roof. They were not the measured tread of a watchman doing his rounds, but of someone in a hurry.

They passed beneath him and on towards the quay. He glimpsed a tall, elderly man moving with a quick, decisive step. He watched, waiting impatiently.

He had almost made up his mind that the coast was clear

when he saw something which made him duck down again. He was almost certain there was a shadowy figure flitting along silently, threateningly, behind the first.

As the elderly man passed the corner of the shed, two other men leapt out in front, barring his way, while the shadow closed in behind. There was a thud and a one-sided struggle started.

"Another Silverman mob," Chip muttered. "Three against one's just about their odds."

The elderly man was giving a good account of himself, but his three assailants gradually backed him towards the shed wall.

Chip hesitated, his quick fury at the unfairness of the attack battling with his reluctance to get mixed up in more trouble. Then, he darted along the roof till he was over the milling figures. The elderly man was being pinned against the wall by two of his attackers, while the third, much smaller than the others, hovered in front.

"Tenez-le," hissed the small man, and with an easy, practised movement, produced a knife from his sleeve. The long blade glittered in the half light.

Chip recoiled at the sight of the steel, but only for an instant. Then his anger overcame his fear. He had had more than he could stomach of one-sided fights.

As the knife was raised, he jumped. His feet crashed on to the shoulders of the small man and they collapsed together in a tangled heap.

Encouraged by this sudden intervention, the elderly man struggled free and let out a shout for help.

The next few moments were too confused for Chip to remember clearly. There was a sickening blow on his head as he saw the small man scramble to his feet and make off. As he went, the small man turned back to shake his fist. That was the one thing that fixed itself in Chip's memory, the sight of the small man silhouetted against the quay lights, his ears standing out from his head like a bat's, shaking his fist with uncontrollable rage.

"You see, Mandrake," screamed the small man. "You see, you will never arrive to the island alive."

Chip stared blankly after the disappearing figure, and then passed clean out.

He had vague memories of being picked up and carried, of strong lights shining in his face, of a furious argument nearby, and then darkness again.

When he recovered his senses, he slowly became aware that he was on a bed in a small room, stripped of his out-door clothes.

Someone, bending over him, was saying: "Looks a bit white, Purser. Sensitive face. Interesting lad. What do you think? Is he going to be all right?"

A voice farther off, replied: "Slight concussion, I'd say, Dr. Mandrake. He'll be as fit as a fiddle in a day or two."

Chip opened his eyes fully to find himself staring up into the face of the elderly man. A long, narrow face it was, with a high, domed forehead above fierce eyes. The white hair, flaring eyebrows and trim beard were shot with iron grey. It was an impatient face, but for the moment it wore an expression of concern.

"He's coming out of it," said the elderly man, and then to Chip: "Lie still, boy. You're all right. Quite safe."

"Just let him lie here for a while, Dr. Mandrake," said the other man. Out of the corner of his eye Chip could just see a blue uniform with some gold braid. "Then I'll get a taxi to take him home, or maybe the police will do it."

"Police!" barked the elderly man. "After what they let happen to me! Certainly not, indeed no! In any case, what was this boy up to in the docks? No good, I'll be bound. They'd want to know about it. Leave him here, Purser, I'll see to him."

"Very good, sir. I'd be glad. I'm very busy before sailing."

"Now," said the bearded man to Chip when they were alone. "How do you feel, boy? What's your name?"

"My head hurts," said Chip ruefully. "And my name's Wood, Charles Wood."

"Very well, Charles Wood, my name's Mandrake, and I'm indebted to you. You saved me a good deal of trouble to-night. You may have saved my life. What were you doing in the docks?"

"Well," began Chip. His head was throbbing and he could not think clearly. "It's my birthday. I'm fifteen to-day . . . Where is this . . .?"

"An excellent reason. You climb about dock roofs to celebrate birthdays, do you? Never mind, you're still dazed. We're in my cabin on the motor vessel *Salamander*. Not due to sail for several hours, so you can rest here for a while. Then I'll see you get home safely. I've got a lot to do myself, so if you're comfortable for the moment, I'll leave you." He turned off the light and hesitated at the door, then he came back and put his hand on Chip's shoulder. "The police caught two of the men, the other two got away. Thought you would like to know. You did a courageous thing, boy," he said gruffly. "I'm grateful."

Chip still felt dazed and in any case he often felt drowsy after he had been worked up like to-night. He lay staring at the reflection of the dock lights on the ceiling. He felt he could lie there for ever, safe, warm and enclosed, with no bothers about Silverman, no aunt screaming at him, no dreary streets lined with grey houses and factories, just the soft bunk, semi-darkness, and distant hum of machines somewhere in the ship, dulling the ache in his head.

His eyelids drooped.

He had an idea that someone was moving about nearby. He half-opened his eyes. A man in a white jacket was standing on the other side of the cabin, adjusting a ventilator. A small man he was, and he was placing a box in the open shaft. Chip watched him close the grille. It did not matter, he was obviously a steward. Chip felt uneasy for a moment, then closed his eyes again and let himself drift luxuriously until he slipped into a deep sleep.

But something bothered and disturbed him so that his sleep became fitful and restless, full of confused dreams. Silverman's face smiled triumphantly at him, followed by his aunt talking her head off, but without uttering a sound. She kept opening and shutting her mouth silently, like a goldfish. Then he saw the small man on the dock with the knife, running away with his ears standing out more than ever, so that he looked like a chimpanzee. Although the small figure ran faster and faster, it never seemed to get any farther off, and it was wearing a white jacket, like the steward, just like the steward. In fact . . .

Chip woke up with a start that nearly jolted him off the bunk. That was who the steward reminded him of: the small man with the knife. It had been the protruding ears that had made him look familiar.

Still not properly awake, Chip staggered from the bunk over to the ventilator. He must have been more badly hurt than he had thought, because he could hardly keep his feet. He caught sight of his reflection in a wall mirror. He did not look too bad, rather rumpled perhaps. His hair, dry now, was tangled like a mat, but no more than usual when he got out of bed. A bit pale, so that his freckles stood out, but on the whole he looked in order. His eyes were puffy and half-closed. He tried to rub the sleep out of them before fumbling with the catch of the ventilator grille. Then he was standing there with a wooden box in his hand, staring at it stupidly.

In that instant, all trace of sleep left him. He realised that it was not he who was staggering, but the whole cabin. And it was no longer dark, for grey light was filtering through the portholes. He dashed over and stared out, to be confronted with a wide expanse of stormy water. The fog had completely gone, driven away by the rising wind. The coastline lay far astern, low on the horizon. It was too far off to distinguish any buildings or other features. The *Salamander* was already so far out that, he could see from the curving wake, she was bearing round on a course parallel to the coast. She was pitching so violently that he went back and sat down on the bunk.

He had obviously slept much longer than he had thought, and in the fuss of sailing, everyone must have overlooked the fact that he was aboard.

He thought about his aunt and the row there was going to be. By this time she would have gone to the police. He had never stayed out all night before.

Then he forgot all about his aunt, the police, and his other troubles. For the box he had found in the ventilator had started ticking.

CHAPTER TWO

A SMALL MAN

THE TICKING persisted, a harsh metallic sound like that of a cheap alarm clock. He turned the box over cautiously. The lid was securely fastened so that he could not see inside. On the bottom was a cross and skull stencilled in black. He had read and heard enough about the war to recognise German weapon marks. If the steward was the small man with the knife, then he must have been trying to carry out his threat that Dr. Mandrake would not arrive at some island alive. Chip did not wait to see any more. There was only one thing to do, throw the box into the sea before it exploded.

The porthole was securely screwed down and would not budge when he tugged at it, so he grabbed the box from the bed and dashed out into the companionway, forgetting that he was still in his underclothes.

He scrambled up a flight of stairs, hanging on grimly to the handrail as the ship buried its prow in the heavy seas. He shouldered open a steel door on to the deserted deck. The wind tore at him so that he could hardly breathe as he fought his way to the side. He stood poised for a second, then flung the box as far as he could. The wind caught it and carried it astern, away from the ship.

At the second of impact it burst, loosing a yellow cloud. He heard nothing above the roar of the wind.

"Gas!" he muttered. "That's what it was, poison gas." He stood there, staring, until, with a shiver, he realised that the icy spray had soaked him to the skin.

The first thing to do was to dress, and the second to find Mandrake.

As he turned to go below, he was confronted by Mandrake himself and another man, battling their way across the deck towards him.

Mandrake flung a coat around him, shouted something that was lost in the wind, and half-led, half-dragged him along the deck to the saloon.

"I thought you were going over the side, Charles Wood," gasped Mandrake when they were inside. "For one ghastly moment I thought you were going to try swimming ashore."

The other man called to a steward Chip had not seen before for a travelling rug, and having wrapped Chip in it, fetched a mug of steaming coffee.

"Drink this," he said, in a soft, guttural voice. "What made you do such a foolish thing? Who are you, anyway? I did not see there were any children on board when I studied the passenger list."

Before Chip could reply, Mandrake broke in:

"My fault, guilty of a ridiculous oversight. Checking my baggage and equipment, entirely forgot to have you put ashore. In fact, it slipped my mind until I saw you appear on deck."

"Is this the boy who assisted you when you were attacked?" asked the other man, and Chip caught a foreign intonation in his tone.

"Indeed, yes," said Mandrake. "Ashamed to say, Mr. Kreamer, that I rewarded him by forgetting his existence. Unforgivable."

"And now it is too late, for the pilot has already been taken off, otherwise this boy could have gone ashore with him," added Kreamer.

Mandrake jumped to his feet. He seemed a very energetic

and impulsive man, in spite of his age. He was erect and wiry too.

"Must find the purser at once. See what can be done to get you ashore, Charles Wood."

Chip set down his cup of coffee. "Dr. Mandrake, I must tell you, I think one of the men who attacked you is on the ship. He put a bomb in your cabin. I threw it overboard, that's what . . ."

"A bomb!" echoed Mandrake. "A *bomb!* Absurd! Why should . . .?"

"Perhaps this boy has imagined it," put in Kreamer.

"No," protested Chip indignantly. "It exploded. I saw it explode when it hit the water."

Mandrake looked down at him, his eyes narrowed with surprise and disbelief. He did not reply directly, but said: "Must see the purser, then we will go down to my cabin again."

"You have imagined this, perhaps," said Kreamer when Mandrake had left them. "Why should anyone wish to hurt the distinguished doctor. Do you know? He does no harm exploring and digging up ruins."

Chip flushed and stared resentfully at Kreamer. Often he felt uncertain of himself and when, like now, he was sure of his ground he could not bear contradiction. Kreamer was an odd-looking man, squat and powerful with an unexpected agility in his movements. But it was his eyes that riveted Chip's attention. They were pale, so pale they looked like faded bits of blue glass stuck in his skull. They were cold and unfeeling, untouched by the smile Kreamer was wearing. The pupils were like pinpoints of darkness, fixed and unblinking.

Chip looked away uncomfortably.

"I don't know Dr. Mandrake, or why anyone should

want to kill him," he muttered sullenly. "But it's true, what I'm saying."

"I was not suggesting that you were making it up. But you had a blow on the head, yes? This may have caused you to connect the man on the quay with the steward. Would you recognise the steward again?"

Chip hesitated. Kreamer laughed, as though that settled the matter.

"Better forget it. You cannot accuse people unless you are sure. Probably the box you threw overboard was part of Dr. Mandrake's equipment. Nothing important, let us hope."

He stood up, swaying easily with the motion of the ship. "I too have my affairs to deal with. We shall meet later, Charles." Chip chewed his finger tensely. The suggestion that he had imagined the bomb disgusted him. Then he sneezed and drew the rug more tightly around him, shivering in spite of the warmth in the saloon.

While he was waiting for Mandrake to return, he looked about him curiously. The steward had disappeared and he was alone. He had often wondered what the ships in the docks were like, but had never been on one before. This was obviously a cargo boat with accommodation for a few passengers. Pretty luxurious it was, too. Thick carpets, deep padded chairs, indirect lighting, and a faint, expensive smell of cigars. Chip shut his eyes and tried to relax. This was the life all right. He wondered what the ship's destination was. He did not care much, it was out of his hands. Anywhere would be better than going back to the docks and his aunt. He was sorry for her, really, when he thought about it. She had a tough enough time with her own family, without bothering with him. She was always tired and ready to fly off the handle over every little thing. But it was no fun, particularly now that Silverman was after him.

"Asleep, boy?"

Chip looked up, to see that Mandrake had returned.

"Bad news, Charles Wood," said the doctor. "I've seen the captain. No chance of getting you back to land. Weather's too bad for a boat to put out. You will have to stay on board—at least until farther down the coast. If the wind dies down, go ashore at Plymouth. Very sorry, my fault. I'm a fool. No excuse."

An idea had been forming in Chip's mind.

"I . . . I suppose you couldn't give me a job, sir," he blurted out. "Then you wouldn't have to bother about putting me ashore at all."

The doctor's eyebrows shot up.

"A job?" he echoed. "Upon my soul! Well, really, boy. I should be accused of kidnapping you. Out of the question. Besides, what could I do with you? I haven't a job to give you."

Chip remembered what Kreamer had said.

"Are you going on an expedition, sir? Mr. Kreamer said you were an explorer and dug up ruins. Couldn't I come with you? I could look after the baggage and stores. I could be useful, honest, sir."

"Stop, stop, boy," protested the doctor irritably. "I don't know what Mr. Kreamer told you. Not his business anyhow. Quite impossible, Charles Wood." He stared at Chip's disappointed face, and added more sympathetically: "After all, what about your parents?"

"They were killed in a train crash in Lewisham a few years back, and I live with my aunt, sir. She wouldn't mind. I know she wouldn't. In fact she'd be glad to be shot of me, I reckon."

The sudden bitterness in his voice brought a sharp look from Mandrake. Before he knew it, Chip was telling the whole story. It was always like that, keeping everything to himself until he met someone he felt he could trust. Then it all came out in one great burst. The doctor listened gravely until it was finished.

"This Silverman. Yes, I see your problem. There are many Silvermans about. Sounds very much like the vice-chancellor of a university I once belonged to. You say they call you 'Chip,' eh, Charles Wood?"

"Because my name's Wood, you see, sir. Chip Wood."

"Well, Chip, I'm in a difficult position, aren't I? If I took you with me I'd be responsible for you. I'd have to look after you."

"Oh, no, sir," said Chip eagerly. "I can look after myself. Perhaps . . . I . . . could be useful, too."

"You were going to say, perhaps you could look after me. That's what you were going to say, isn't it?" The doctor's fierce eyes twinkled briefly. "Maybe you are right. I'll think this over. Never make hasty decisions. Weigh everything up, that's the scientific method." He frowned again. "You've a temperature boy. I can see it. Better get the ship's doctor to look at you. Go and get in bed at once."

Chip sneezed twice, as though to confirm this opinion. "Yes, I do feel rather hot," he admitted. "But aren't you a doctor?"

"Yes, yes, of philosophy. Not a medical man. Not the same thing at all. Go and do as you are told, boy. And give me your aunt's address. We must let her know you're safe. Wretched woman must think you've run off, or some such thing. Oh, yes, something else, boy: stop biting your fingers. It annoys me."

Chip went slowly back to the cabin. The deck was still deserted apart from a couple of seamen checking the hatches. Apparently the bad weather was keeping everyone below.

As he was climbing back into the bunk, a sudden thought struck him.

"I must be daft," he muttered. "I never even asked where we're going." But he did not really care, all he wanted to do was shut his eyes again and forget the chill that was making him ache all over. In a few minutes he was fast asleep.

He must have slept for a long time. When he awoke it was already dark. The curtain was drawn across the porthole and the lights were on. Mandrake was sitting in an arm-chair reading some papers.

Chip lay quietly studying him unobserved. The doctor's thin, narrow face was set in concentration. The table light made his white hair glow softly, giving him a benign appearance that was offset by the sharp glint of his half-spectacles and by his rather tart expression. It was difficult to believe that he was mixed up in anything shady or that anyone was trying deliberately to kill him. In spite of the brusque manner, Chip instinctively trusted him.

Mandrake glanced over his spectacles:

"Ah, you're awake then. Feel better? Good. I've more news for you. The doctor had a look at you while you were asleep. You must stay in bed for several days."

"In bed," echoed Chip. Then he realised what this meant. "You're going to take me with you, Dr. Mandrake?"

"Your aunt has given her permission over the wireless," said the doctor. "So I've decided to take you with me, yes. Hope I shall not regret it. You're impetuous, Chip. Don't know where we're going, or what we shall be doing when we get there, do you?"

Chip grinned:

"I don't really care either, sir. I've always wanted to travel, go on a ship."

"Certainly going to travel. Destination's an island off the coast of South America. I have work to do there."

"Digging up some ruins?"

Mandrake winced. "*Not* digging up. Makes me sound like a dog with a bone. Investigating part of an ancient city—a scientific investigation. Hard work; long, tiring, hard work. Don't ask if there will be buried treaure. There won't be. You *can* be useful. Intended taking an assistant, but he broke a leg—playing rugby—young fool. You've no training, but you can learn, can't you? Have to work, you know."

"Yes, I'll try," said Chip with such determination that the doctor nodded approvingly.

"You can start with this, then," he said, tossing a thin leather-bound volume on to the bed. "Reference book about the island. Tell you something of the history, the people, and so forth. Read it. Any questions, ask me."

Chip picked it up and read the title aloud: "*The Island of the Four Apostles.*" Underneath in smaller letters this was repeated in French, which he followed less confidently. "*L'Île des Quatre Apôtres* by Jean Paul Periot, translated from the French by Henry Mandrake, Sedley Professor of Archæology, Layfield University." He looked up inquiringly. "Is that you, Dr. Mandrake?"

Mandrake nodded: "Indeed, yes," he said.

"It's a funny name for an island, the Four Apostles."

"It comes from four hills at the north of the island. Frenchman called de Malpré was shipwrecked there nearly two hundred years ago. Named the hills and the island after the apostles in gratitude for being saved from the sea. Turned the place into a French colony, but it became independent after the Revolution."

"Are there any natives?" asked Chip hopefully.

"Certainly; splendid people called the Gardiens. You'll

find their story in the book. They keep very much to themselves in the forests and mountains in the south of the island. Used to be friendly with the French settlers, in fact de Malpré married one of them. Then they quarrelled, many years ago."

"What about?"

Mandrake frowned and stood up. He had seemed to have settled down to give a lecture, but now thought better of it.

"Read the book, boy. It's all there. Usual story, greed in the name of progress. French tried to turn the Gardiens into slaves to work the copper. Rich in copper, the island. But the Gardiens weren't having any, very proud, very fierce people. In the end the French had to get natives from South America and leave the Gardiens to themselves. Read the book, though. That's why I gave it to you!" He started collecting together the papers he had been reading. "I've engaged another cabin next door. I'll be there. Will you be all right?"

Chip nodded comfortably. "I'll be fine Dr. Mandrake—and thanks for taking me with you. I'll work hard, honest, I will."

Mandrake grunted doubtfully. "Very well, then. Any other questions before I go?"

Chip hesitated, then blurted out: "Someone *is* trying to kill you, Dr. Mandrake. It's true, isn't it?"

Mandrake glanced at him sharply, then busied himself with his papers again. "Don't dramatise things, boy," he snapped. "It was attempted robbery at the docks, nothing more. Could have happened to anyone."

Chip flushed. "What about the bomb then?"

"Probably a device for making smoke signals. Ships carry that sort of thing, can't imagine why, but they do. Jumping to conclusions. Unscientific. You must stop it."

Mandrake seemed quite put out. Without giving Chip the chance to question him further he stalked from the cabin in a huff.

Chip picked up his book and stared at the door uneasily. Mandrake was not a man able to conceal his feelings successfully. He was well aware that someone was following him with the deliberate intention of taking his life. Chip was certain of it.

CHAPTER THREE

THE LEGEND

FOR THE NEXT few days the weather continued bad, and Chip was confined to his cabin. Apart from occasional visits from the ship's doctor, a surly man named Roberts, who obviously thought him a nuisance, and from Mandrake, the only one he saw was a steward called Scott, who brought his meals. Scott was tall and cheerful, as unlike the grotesque small man as he could be. He was never able to stop and talk for long, because several of the other passengers were laid up by the rough sea and had to be waited on—like babies, according to him.

He dashed in and out to deliver or collect the tray, giving a few snippets of information in a soft, West Country burr as he came and went.

"It's a dog's life, son," he said good humouredly. "We're always popping to and fro across the Atlantic. South America—London—West Indies—Liverpool. Now we're off to this French island place. It's a dog's life at sea, I tell you."

"Have you been there before, Scotty?" demanded Chip eagerly. "Do you know it?"

"Twice I've been there, not for long, mind. It looks pretty enough, but it's a rough old place by all accounts. The natives have a bad time of it. They're treated like dirt. Everything's run by a big mining company. They run the Government, too, so I've been told. Lot of slave-drivers, they are." He was on his way again without waiting for more questions.

Chip frowned. What he had just heard did not fit in
with what he had been reading. According to the book the
island was, if not prosperous, at least without serious
problems and the natives were reasonably content under
the president, a descendant of the discoverer, de Malpré. Of
course the book was not new. It had been written about
fifteen years before, and things change in such a long time.
Chip grinned, after all *he* had changed quite a bit in fifteen
years.

He picked the book up again and flicked through the
pages. Much of it, on trade and history was pretty dull,
but there was one part, the legend of the Gardiens, which
fascinated him. It was a rather sinister little story. This
would be the third time he had read it. He settled himself
comfortably:

The Legend of the Flashing Mountain
(an account of the myth of the Gardiens)

"When the world was newly created, the god Xarpata chose
the island as his home, and roamed as he pleased across the
plains, in the forests, and among the mountain peaks. He
chose the people of the island as his servants, and he cared
for them, watching over their crops and herds. He
gave them rain and sunshine so that their harvests were
rich and their cattle fat. Although the people were his
servants, they were also his friends, and brought him all
their joys and sorrows, their laughter and their tears,
to share. Xarpata loved his people and they respected
him.

Then Xarpata decided to marry. Being a god, one wife
was not enough for him, so he took two, one brown from
the east and the other white from the west. Both were
beautiful and good and both were equally loved by Xarpata.
For a time he was more happy than ever before, and the

island became like a paradise, echoing with laughter and singing from sunrise to sunset.

But alas, this happiness was not to last, for like a shadow, jealousy came between the white and brown wives. They both suspected that Xarpata preferred the other, and no matter how much he protested that he loved them equally, their suspicions increased, until their affection for each other turned to hatred. At first an angry glance, a bitter word, then soon their voices were raised, shrill with accusation and complaint.

Xarpata's hopes that the discord would soon pass and be replaced by former happiness were disappointed. Instead the quarrels became more frequent and violent.

This caused the people great concern, for Xarpata was neglecting his duties and their crops had withered and their cattle sickened.

They discussed among themselves what they should do, and agreed to send their leader to speak with Xarpata. This he did, saying: 'Oh, Xarpata, all powerful, we are your servants. We were happy in this land you gave us until you took these wives. Now they disturb your peace and our crops wither and our cattle sicken. Put these wives from you, and we shall be happy as we were before.'

Xarpata thought for a long while, and then replied: 'This is well said, O man. This is what I will do. When next my sister the Moon hides her face, I will bury these two wives who disturb my peace, one in one part of the island, and the other in another. Then I will come up into these mountains and hide myself here, and you and your people shall guard me and keep me in peace.'

'We will swear to do this, O Xarpata, and after us, our children,' said the leader of the people.

'If any stranger comes before me to disturb me,' went on Xarpata, 'I shall look at him, and he shall surely die, and if you do not guard me well I shall look at you, and you shall die, with your children, your cattle, and your crops.'

And this is how it came about. When next the moon was dark, Xarpata took his wives while they were sleeping, and buried them, each in a different part of the island. Then Xarpata went up into the mountains and hid himself in a great pillar of rock. There his servants have guarded him to this day, taking for themselves a name which the French settlers translated as 'Les Gardiens.' It is said that if a stranger comes near to disturb him, Xarpata looks at him and he dies. The quarrelling wives were never seen or heard again. They lie buried for all time in widely separated hills in the island, no one knows where."

"That showed 'em," grinned Chip approvingly, but his grin faded. He knew that chapter almost by heart. It left him with an uncomfortable feeling that it meant something he could not understand. It was not until much later that he realised he had the key to a great mystery in his hands. But there were some questions he wanted answers to.

He slipped on the dressing-gown that Scott had lent him, and went out to Mandrake's cabin. The door was ajar, which was lucky, for now that they were well out in the Atlantic and far to the south, the weather was warmer and the doctor spent much of his time on deck.

Chip knocked and pushed open the door. Then he stopped dead in his tracks, for on the far side of the cabin, bending over some cases of equipment, was a steward, a small man with projecting ears. At the sound of Chip's entry, he sprung round. His wizened face was vicious and sly. The hastily assumed smile did not improve it much either.

"You look for Dr. Mandrake, Monsieur?" the steward asked sharply. His left eye twitched continually in a mirthless, nervous wink. "He is not here. I saw him on the sun deck a few moments ago. The doctor wanted his glasses, and asked me to bring them to him. So!" He held up Mandrake's binoculars.

Chip stared and stood aside silently to let him pass. As he looked after the slight figure he could have sworn that this was the man he had seen in the docks and in the cabin the first night aboard. He had not imagined those projecting ears, or, come to think of it, the French accent either.

He decided to question Scott more persistently the next time he saw him. Up to now he had had no luck when he had asked about the small steward. Scott had said that as this was the Frenchman's first voyage, there had been no time to get to know him well.

Recovering his breath, Chip felt angry with himself for being so unnerved. He decided to check up to see if anything had been disturbed or tampered with. He was quite sure he had not imagined about the bomb, either, so he first tried the ventilator, but the grille was firmly in place, and in fact had been painted over. Then he looked at the equipment boxes. They were long and narrow with the words "Fragile" and "Handle with care" stencilled on them. The lid of the top one was open. Chip knew that Mandrake would never be guilty of such carelessness. He guarded the boxes as though they contained the Crown jewels or dynamite, or something. That was why they were in his cabin, instead of being stowed with the other baggage. His curiosity aroused, Chip stared inside. What he saw made him whistle softly. He did not know what equipment an archæologist needed to excavate ancient cities, but he had never imagined that delicate and complicated electronic gadgets would be necessary. That was what the top box contained. There was nothing that he could even faintly recognise, other than a bank of valves and dials. He bent down for a closer look.

He was so intent he did not hear the cabin door open again.

"Do you usually pry in this fashion, Charles Wood?" snapped the familiar voice of Mandrake. "I had not expected this of you."

Chip flushed.

"I wasn't prying," he protested. "But I caught someone who was."

"Who?"

"The steward. The one who tried to kill you in the docks, and put a bomb in your cabin."

Mandrake sat down on his bunk and looked at Chip searchingly.

"Are you sure of this? Quite sure?"

"Well, I'm pretty certain, Dr. Mandrake. He said you had sent him for your binoculars, but he was having a look in this box."

Mandrake thought for a moment, his eyes still on Chip's face.

"If I took you to the captain, could you positively identify this man as the one who attacked me in London. Very dark, you know. Have to be certain. Could not be sure myself."

Chip hesitated.

"Well, *I'm* sure, but I hadn't seen his face before. I remember him clearly putting that bomb . . ."

"Yes, the bomb. Perhaps there was a bomb after all. I have given the matter much thought. I'll be frank with you, Chip. Until recently I'd believed the bomb was your imagination. You'd had a severe blow on the head and were running a high temperature. I may have been unjust to you."

"It *was* a bomb, Dr. Mandrake, honest. I saw it go off," insisted Chip. "In any case I couldn't have imagined that he was French, could I?"

Mandrake smiled ruefully.

"Looks as though I *do* need you to look after me, though why I should need anyone to look after me, I don't know. I just don't know. This small man again. It's true I sent him for my binoculars, but only after he suggested he should get them for me. To see a shoal of flying fish, he said. But I was not able to see them. Very disturbing."

He sat lost in thought until Chip was afraid that he had been forgotten.

"I've finished the book you gave me, Dr. Mandrake," he said conversationally to break the silence. "You said to tell you when I had."

Mandrake stared at him blankly for a moment.

"Good, good," he muttered. "We must talk about it."

"Is all this equipment needed when you dig up ruins?" went on Chip determinedly. Mandrake did not reply at once, but sat, still silently thinking. Then he seemed to make up his mind about something.

"Sit down, Chip," he said, suddenly brisk. "Going to be completely frank with you. Some things you should know. Only fair. Julius may have been right, perhaps there is danger. Perhaps there was a bomb. But you must keep this to yourself, absolutely. I told you the purpose of my visit to the Island of the Four Apostles, to excavate an ancient city. Quite true. But the reason why I'm going at this particular time is to visit a friend, a very old friend. Have you ever heard of Julius Schumann?"

"No," replied Chip. "I've never heard of him."

Mandrake looked surprised and rather shocked at such ignorance.

"Most distinguished physicist in Germany before the war. Had to escape from the Nazis. Went to America and helped develop the atomic bomb. When he realised what a ghastly weapon it was, he gave it all up and retired to this island."

"And you are just going to see him?" asked Chip rather disappointedly. It did not seem to be much to make a fuss about.

"I'm taking this equipment to him," replied Mandrake. "Wrote and asked me to do so. Said it was a matter of the greatest urgency. In fact, he said it was a matter of life and death. It is of this I have been thinking. Julius is not given to exaggeration, a fine scientist."

"What's it for, Dr. Mandrake?"

"Julius did not explain in his letter. Hinted it was for a discovery he had made. This I do not understand because he has no laboratory and is no longer working. I am not a physicist, so these gadgets mean little to me. I cannot say."

"What's a physicist do?" asked Chip.

Mandrake stroked his beard absently. "Well . . . he's a scientist who studies the—er—physical nature of things. It's a wide subject."

"Doesn't help much then, does it, Dr. Mandrake?" said Chip, still puzzled.

"Strange letter, unlike Julius. He hinted strongly that there was great danger but he was most cautious, as though expecting the letter to be read by someone else besides me. First the attack at the docks, then someone tampering with the equipment—perhaps it was a bomb after all," repeated Mandrake for the third time, then relapsed into uneasy silence.

Chip waited for a while, then seeing that Mandrake had completely forgotten about him, decided that this was not the time to discuss the book, and crept from the cabin.

CHAPTER FOUR

THE DISASTROUS MISTAKE

CHIP THOUGHT a good deal about what Mandrake had told him, even though he found plenty to do during the next few days. Dr. Roberts declared him fit again, and allowed him up on deck, where he quickly made friends with some of the crew.

There were only six other passengers, mostly business people, and, with the exception of Kreamer, they kept very much to themselves. Kreamer became very familiar and went out of his way to make the voyage interesting. He arranged for conducted tours of the engine-room and the radio centre, and even persuaded the captain to take Chip on to the bridge, which was apparently a great privilege.

Chip felt a bit guilty about it, but he could not like Kreamer, whose friendliness somehow seemed out of keeping with the watchfulness of his cold, pale eyes. Chip had the uncomfortable feeling that he was being pumped about Mandrake, who no longer came on deck, but spent most of his time writing in his cabin, shut up with his equipment.

"You are indeed fortunate to be befriended by such a distinguished man, Chip," said Kreamer one evening when they were on deck together. "You will find it interesting to work on the ancient city of the Gardiens with him."

"You know about it, Mr. Kreamer? Have you ever seen it?"

"Alas, no. This is my first visit to the island of the Four

38

Apostles and I am on business. But we Germans are a great race for archæology. There are many famous German archæologists who have done important work and developed very special ways of measuring their discoveries." Kreamer laughed gently. "Did you know that you can tell the age of old bones, for example, by the amount of radioactivity in them?"

"No," said Chip, feeling there was a double purpose in this question. "I don't know much about it."

"It is possible," continued Kreamer. "I should like to discuss this with Dr. Mandrake. I wonder if it is a method he uses."

Chip was saved the trouble of saying again that he did not know, by the appearance of Scott.

"Wireless, Mr. Kreamer," said the steward, handing Kreamer one of two yellow envelopes he was carrying. Kreamer took it without a word of thanks, and abruptly turned his back before opening the message. Scott winked at Chip and made off. That was one thing that Chip had noticed about Kreamer. He never bothered to be civil to any of the crew, but treated them as if they were part of the furniture. Kreamer crammed the message in his pocket, swung round, pushed Chip aside, and strode swiftly after Scott. Chip stared after him, taken aback by the sudden change of mood, for Kreamer's stony eyes had become alight with blazing anger.

Chip hesitated for a moment, then decided to follow. He was curious to know what Kreamer's interest in Mandrake was, and wondered whether what had just happened might provide a clue. He slipped silently to the companionway down which Kreamer had disappeared. It looked as though the German was returning to his cabin and Chip knew that the best vantage point would be the narrow strip of deck outside. As the weather was calm and they were approaching the tropics, most of the passengers had had their portholes unbolted and left open. With luck, Chip thought, he might be able to see what Kreamer was doing. But he was disappointed, for the porthole was well above his head, and he could hardly climb up for a look without being seen.

The deck was deserted except for some of the engine-room staff who were snatching a breath of fresh air, so Chip leaned against the rail as if he were watching the sunset.

He heard the door slam in Kreamer's cabin and wondered whether the German had gone out again, but a second later he pricked up his ears.

"You rang, Monsieur?" It was the unmistakable voice of the French steward.

"You are Louis Petit, aren't you?" asked Kreamer.

There was silence for a moment, and when the steward replied all the servility had gone from his voice.

"What are you? Police?"

"You might say police," agreed Kreamer. "But not the police you are afraid of. I'm going to the island to take charge of the Syndicate's police. Do you understand?"

There was another pause before the steward replied.

"Why did you not tell me this before? We could have . . ."

"It amused me not to," said Kreamer. "Watching you and wondering what you would do next about Mandrake. But not any more. Read this!"

Chip guessed that he was handing over the wireless message.

"Fools," snapped Kreamer. "It is clearly time I arrived to take charge. I take charge here, now. You understand. Now! You do as I say. After this disastrous mistake, Mandrake must not be harmed. We may need him. You do not touch him. This is clear?"

"I have my orders, too," complained Petit.

"Orders! You take my orders. Mandrake must not be touched. Up to now, what you did about him I did not care. But now there must be no more mistakes. That is all."

"I suppose the Gestapo never made mistakes," sneered Petit.

When Kreamer spoke again his voice was so quiet that Chip had to strain to hear what he said.

"Do not speak of the Gestapo, Petit. That was a long time ago. But I have not forgotten what I learnt there. If you are impertinent to me, I will show you. Now get out!"

Chip scuttled away. He did not want to be around if Petit came out on to the deck. He made straight for Mandrake's cabin.

He found the doctor sitting on his bunk looking pale and shaken. As Chip poured out his story he listened in silence, until the Gestapo was mentioned.

"Do you know what that was, Chip?" he asked.

"Well, not exactly," admitted Chip.

"It was the German Nazi Police. The vilest set of men who ever existed. They did unspeakable things."

"But I thought that sort of thing finished at the end of the war," said Chip.

"Yes. Many of them paid on the gallows for what they did. Not all, of course. Some are still free, with false identities. Kreamer must be one of those."

"But what does it all mean, Dr. Mandrake? Why do they want to kill you?"

"Don't know. Just don't know." Mandrake sounded tired and dispirited. His usually erect shoulders were bowed as though he was carrying a great weight. "But I can guess what the blunder was that Kreamer was talking about."

"Yes?" asked Chip. "What?"

Mandrake held up the yellow form of a wireless message and Chip guessed that it must have been the second one that Scott had been carrying.

"Just had this from the hospital in S. Jean, the capital of the island. Julius Schumann was taken there early to-day. Been shot three times. He died two hours ago."

CHAPTER FIVE

THE ISLAND OF THE FOUR APOSTLES

"CAN YOU see it, Chip? The hill of S. Jean, straight ahead
Over to the left, the hill of S. Luc. Can't see the others,
they're too far off."

Chip followed the direction in which Mandrake was
pointing across the sun-drenched sea. He could just make
out the crest of the two hills on the horizon. Above them
towered a high bank of cumulus cloud, brilliantly white
against the tropical sky.

Chip watched fascinated as the *Salamander* sliced her way
through the lazy swell. The island of the Four Apostles
looked as colourful and promising as any tropical island he
had read about. Mandrake must have sensed what Chip
was thinking, for he smiled rather sourly.

"Beautiful, beautiful, is it not? It's inhabited, that's the
trouble with it, though. There are people there. They
spoil anything, given the chance."

But Chip was not so easily put off. His serious face relaxed
in a grin as native twin-boomed fishing craft, with
bright orange sails, swooped so close across their bows
that the *Salamander's* siren thundered a warning over the
bay.

"What's that on the top of S. Jean, Dr. Mandrake?" he
demanded, pointing to a group of low buildings capping the
hill. A castellated wall with embrasures reached down the
precipitous slope to the water's edge. A flag hung listlessly
over the largest of the group. The great dark mass capping

the hill seemed to brood oppressively over the activity and bright colours in the harbour.

"President's palace. Built by the first governor, fortified by his sons," said Mandrake. "Meant to protect the town and harbour. Who it protects now, I don't know. Probably the President from his loyal citizens."

He sounded so sour that Chip glanced at him. Mandrake's long thin face looked stern and intent. He had thrown off the lethargy that had overtaken him on hearing of the death of his friend and had again become brisk and purposeful. He stared up at the palace.

"Going up there, Chip. Directly I heard of Julius Schumann's death I wirelessed the President for an interview. Always go to the man at the top. That's a good rule. I mean to find out what's behind this. Why Julius Schumann was killed, and what he had discovered." He spoke determinedly, as though the death of his friend had finally made up his mind for him.

The soft voice of Kreamer broke in behind them: "May I offer my services, Dr. Mandrake, in helping you through the customs formalities?" The German was immaculate in a light tropical suit. He removed his panama hat and leaned on the rail beside them. He presented a striking and elegant contrast to Mandrake who was wearing a faded khaki bush shirt, slacks and sandals, topped off by a battered, wide-brimmed straw hat. Ever since they had reached the tropics Mandrake's costume had become increasingly disreputable until now only the trimness of his beard and confident, authoritative manner, distinguished him from a beachcomber.

He eyed Kreamer coldly. "Thank you, but I have been here before," he replied shortly, but Kreamer was not so easily discouraged.

"Ah, I was not forgetting. This was ten or fifteen years

ago. Things change, Dr. Mandrake. I have much experience of the official mind. If you have difficulty, I shall be privileged to be of service."

In spite of the courteous words, Chip felt that they concealed a threat. He could not get out of his mind Kreamer's sudden change from affability to fury when he received the wireless message about Schumann's death. Mandrake must have had similar feelings, for he met the German's compelling eyes directly.

"Trust I shall not need help, Mr. Kreamer. But I shall remember your offer."

Kreamer half smiled and turned to Chip.

"Are you excited at your first sight of the island? Perhaps Dr. Mandrake will allow me to show you the sights of the town of S. Jean. This is my first visit and there must be many things to see. It will be an interesting experience for you, too." He pointed to the white walls and coloured roofs, grouped in terraces along the shoulder of the hill of S. Luc.

"Going into the interior almost immediately," cut in Mandrake. "Little time for sightseeing."

Kreamer smiled imperturbably and turned back to the rail.

The *Salamander* swung sharply to avoid a sand bar across the mouth of the great bay, then bore up past two rust-stained ships loading mineral ore from a narrow-gauge mineral railway that ran out from the quay on a ramshackle timber jetty.

Kreamer gave a sharp exclamation. He was looking seawards and Chip followed his gaze. As the bows of the *Salamander* swung towards the quay a magnificent ocean-going yacht in the inner basin came into view. She lay moored a hundred yards or so from the landing-stage, her dazzling white paintwork and polished metal glittering in a thousand reflections from the placid water. Her lines were low and rakish, suggesting power and speed. Above and behind the enclosed bridge were revolving radar navigational aids and a battery of wireless aerials that looked capable of world-wide transmission and reception. Mounted on the afterdeck was a helicopter with the blades of its great rotor folded down for safe storage. Chip gazed, fascinated by this picture of purposeful luxury and strained to catch the name *Midas* across the yacht's stern.

"Perhaps you would like to look, Dr. Mandrake," said Kreamer, who had been studying the *Midas* intently through a pair of binoculars. His tone showed that what he saw gave him satisfaction.

Mandrake grunted and adjusted the focus.

"One would need the golden touch of Midas to maintain it," he said sourly, passing the glasses to Chip. "Can think of better uses for the money."

Chip swept the length of the *Midas*, taking in every detail. The closer view confirmed that no expense had been spared in constructing and equipping the yacht. The only movement on board was the fluttering of a pennant from the stern. It carried the sign of a mailed fist. At first Chip thought she was deserted, but then he spotted a solitary figure in the shadow of an awning across an observation deck forward of the bridge. A short stubby figure it was, dressed in faultless white, standing motionless, arms folded, head slightly bowed, brooding across the water towards the town of S. Jean.

"Did you see him, Dr. Mandrake?" demanded Kreamer, a note of triumph in his voice, as though claiming credit for something.

"I saw him," replied Mandrake shortly. "Malik, wasn't it? Josef Malik? Recognised him from newspaper pictures."

"The richest man in the world," elaborated Kreamer approvingly.

"And one of the most unsavoury," added Mandrake tartly. "Armament manufacturer, warmonger, exploiter of people who cannot defend themselves. The difference between him and King Midas, Mr. Kreamer, is that to get his gold Midas caused suffering mostly to himself. Malik does so by causing misery to others." He stumped disgustedly away across the deck without looking back.

Almost as though he had heard these disparaging remarks, the man on the yacht turned and stared up at the *Salamander* nosing in to her berth. The glasses brought him so close that Chip had the impression of staring directly into his face. It was an old, expressionless face, with heavy lines and dead, lack-lustre eyes. Beneath sleek, well-groomed hair, the face was pallid, like parchment. Josef Malik might be the richest man in the world but it did not seem to Chip that he was enjoying it much.

Kreamer took the binoculars.

"Tell Dr. Mandrake my offer of assistance remains open," he said. "No doubt we shall encounter one another again. It is a small island."

To Chip's relief he did not see Kreamer again until they were ashore. It was tricky landing without tugs, but the captain managed it expertly, with no more trouble than if he had been parking a car. Within seconds of the first hawsers going ashore, ragged native porters were swarming aboard to the passenger quarters, quarrelling loudly among themselves, for luggage.

Mandrake insisted on supervising the unloading of his boxes of equipment himself. Chip heard his voice barking irritably above the chatter of the porters, and decided to keep out of the way. He went back to say good-bye to

Scott, and then followed the doctor down the gangway to the customs.

Although there were only a few passengers to be examined, the long customs hall seemed full of dark-skinned people, shouting and jostling. The heat and noise met him like a wave. He pushed his way through to where Mandrake was standing with his luggage and equipment waiting for a customs officer.

"It's like Hampstead Heath on Bank Holiday, Dr. Mandrake," he grinned.

"No organisation," snapped Mandrake. "Typical. Watch those bags or some thieving rascal will be off with them. Hey! You—yes, you. Come here at once."

A slim man in an olive green uniform appeared on the other side of the customs counter. He saluted and a brilliant smile lit up his bronze features.

"Welcome back to L'Île des Quatre Apôtres, Dr. Mandrake," he shouted in excellent English. "I had the honour to pass you through the customs on your last visit."

"Ah," said Mandrake, taken aback. "Good of you to remember. Just look at my things, there's a good fellow. Like to get out of this appalling noise as soon as may be."

"Not necessary, Dr. Mandrake, to inspect your luggage," replied the customs officer, and leaning over the counter scrawled on the bags and boxes with chalk. But, before he could finish, another officer, this time in a black uniform, appeared, and in spite of protests pushed him roughly aside. The new man was short and burly, with an aggressive manner. His lapel and cap badges were in the form of a mailed fist.

"Put those boxes down," he bawled to the porters. Then he turned to Mandrake. "Now you. Give me your papers."

Mandrake flushed angrily at the offensive tone, but produced his passport without argument.

"Now the boy. Where are his papers?"

"Not here," snapped Mandrake. "Already explained by wireless what has happened and received permission from your Government for this boy to land."

"That's for me to say," shouted the officer. "What's in those boxes?"

"Equipment. Electronic equipment for Professor Schumann."

"Open them. I wish to inspect. They may be subject to duty."

Chip could see the veins in Mandrake's neck swelling with fury. For a moment he thought the doctor would strike the officer, but Mandrake crashed back the lids and contented himself with thrusting out his beard defiantly, as though challenging the man to do his worst.

The officer inspected the intricate equipment, and it was obvious to Chip that he had no idea what it was.

"I shall confiscate this," he announced at length, slamming the lids down again.

This was too much for Mandrake.

"You will do no such thing," he flared. "This is still the property of Layfield University on loan to Professor Schumann. It is not being imported. Don't you know your own regulations?"

"Schumann is dead," retorted the officer, scarlet with anger at having his decision questioned. "The Syndicate allows no electronic equipment into the island without permission. I shall confiscate it and you—you are under arrest for resisting me."

Chip felt himself being pushed aside, and the bulky figure of Kreamer squeezed out of the throng of interested spectators. Even in this oppressive heat he appeared cool and unruffled. He tapped Mandrake's shoulder with the head of his malacca cane.

"You are having trouble, Dr. Mandrake?" he inquired. "What is the matter?"

Mandrake had difficulty in regaining his temper enough to explain.

"This is simply settled," said Kreamer, and, turning to the black-uniformed officer said quietly but distinctly: "Return the doctor's passport and release his luggage."

The officer thumped the counter, almost beside himself.

"You, too, are under arrest," he screamed. "Who are you to give me orders?"

Kreamer leaned across the counter until his face was within inches of the other man's.

"Jason Kreamer," he replied, his voice calm and even. Then suddenly with the speed and viciousness of a snake he slashed the man full across the face with his cane.

A complete hush instantly fell in the long hall, so that the only sound was the swish of the great fans under the roof.

"Jason Kreamer," he repeated. "Remember that. Now give the distinguished doctor back his passport."

The man had shrunk back against the wall, all his bluster gone. Blood trickled between the fingers of the hand he had clapped across his face. He did not move, simply crouched there staring at Kreamer.

"Very well," Kreamer shrugged. "I will return it myself."

He took the passport from the counter and gave it to Mandrake.

"Now, I will see you find transport to your hotel. You see, things *have* changed, Dr. Mandrake."

The crowd of natives melted before Kreamer as he led the way to the exit. Chip saw, by the fear in their faces, that anyone who could treat a black uniform like that and get away with it, was a person of great authority. Even the other uniformed figures guarding the doors stepped smartly aside to let them pass.

"There is your hotel bus," said Kreamer. "I hope your accommodation will be comfortable. If I can be of further assistance to you, do not hesitate to let me know, please. You will always be able to reach me through the offices of the Syndicat International de l'Exploitation des Ressources Naturelles. Quite a mouthful, I'm afraid, but anyone will tell you where it is."

Mandrake drew himself erect. He was obviously disturbed and embarrassed by what had happened.

"Grateful for your help, Kreamer," he said abruptly. "Don't approve of violence. The man was doing his duty, insolently perhaps, but . . ."

Kreamer held up his hand.

"Forgive me, but I understand the official mind, as I have said. I know best how to deal with my people."

"*Your* people?" Mandrake's eyes narrowed. "Are they your people?"

"The officials you see in black uniform belong to the Syndicate, who employ me. Josef Malik is the Chairman of the Syndicate. He was not satisfied with the ability of the President's officials to keep order. He has arranged for a special police force—and has sent for me to take charge of it. I have told you, Dr. Mandrake, there have been changes here in the last ten years."

This exchange was a bit beyond Chip, but he could see that Mandrake was becoming increasingly ill at ease, and that this was causing Kreamer sardonic amusement.

"I assure you that I shall be able to be of great assistance to you. Please do not forget this," smiled Kreamer, and left them before Mandrake could reply.

The doctor was preoccupied and silent as the single-decker bus pulled out from the harbour. Chip did not mind, for he was intent on taking in the unfamiliar sights, noises, and strange spicy smells. Later would be time for questions, but for the moment he was concerned with the town of S. Jean. The streets by the harbour were narrow and congested, thronged with small, dark-skinned people who stood aside as the bus passed with klaxon blaring. Chip noticed their ragged clothes, and blank unsmiling faces, and the many black-uniformed police among them. He noticed, too, that the houses, which from the ship had looked colourful and gay, presented a different appearance close to. The white walls bulged and crumbled, while the roofs sagged with decay and neglect. Here and there the plaster had fallen away, revealing the shoddy construction beneath. Paintwork, bleached by the fierce sun, peeled and flaked from shrivelled wooden frames and shutters. Missing windows were boarded up, and roofs were roughly patched with sailcloth and tarpaulins.

This all seemed depressing enough to Chip as the bus ground up the terraces in low gear, but, even worse, were the children who lurked in doorways and stood sad-eyed in the shadows watching them pass. It just did not seem natural that they should be so quiet and lifeless. He had seen enough people around the docks in London who were badly off, but nothing approaching such poverty as this.

He turned to question Mandrake, and was taken aback by the expression on the doctor's face. Mandrake was glaring out of the window, bristling with anger and astonishment. He caught Chip's eye.

"He was right, boy. Kreamer was right. There have been changes in the last ten years. This is a disgrace. Sheer wanton neglect. Look at them." He stabbed a finger towards some children playing listlessly in a courtyard. "Underfed. That's what it is. Malnutrition. Disgraceful! Only ones with enough to eat are the police." His voice trembled venomously. "White trash. Outcasts from Europe."

Chip had never heard so much feeling in Mandrake's voice before. He looked less like a professor than an avenger, so angry had he become. His grey hair stood out in spikes under his battered hat and his keen eyes glinted fiercely.

As they climbed higher they left the squalid districts behind for larger houses, which in turn gave way to modern villas with commanding views over the bay. Most of them were protected by iron gates, and quite a few had armed sentries outside. Chip noticed that those that were guarded had a small plaque on the gates on which was embossed the now familiar insignia of the mailed fist.

The hotel was at the top of the slope, directly south of the harbour. Seen from this height S. Jean regained some of its romantic appearance, but Chip was not taken in twice.

"Worse than London, Dr. Mandrake," he said.

Mandrake climbed stiffly from the bus.

"Doesn't compare, boy. Don't know what has happened since I last was here. It was a poor enough place then, but now it is degraded. What is this?" Mandrake indicated the hotel entrance which was guarded by the ominous black-uniformed figures. "Like a military camp or a prison." He turned to the native driver. "Is the whole island like this?"

But the native glanced nervously away and pretended not to hear. Mandrake did not press him for a reply.

In contrast to what they had seen in the town, the hotel was a picture of expensive elegance. Chip had never been in such a place before. It was built round an open courtyard, with wide, shady colonnades giving on to a water garden. The vestibule was cool and fresh, air-conditioned and superbly furnished. But whatever impression it made on Chip, it did not please Mandrake. In fact, he was in such a bad humour that clearly nothing would have pleased him. "Vulgar," he snapped, glowering at a brilliant mosaic. "Worst possible taste, the whole thing." All the same he stopped at the hotel shop and insisted on buying some white drill shirts and shorts for Chip, whose wardrobe was restricted to the clothes he had left London in and a few oddments that Scott had found and trimmed down for him on the *Salamander*.

The porter bowed them into their suite, which consisted of two bedrooms and a private lounge.

"What's this? Haven't booked this. Not a millionaire or a profiteer," rapped Mandrake.

"This was reserved for you on the orders of the President's office, Your Excellency," insisted the porter.

Mandrake frowned, thought for a moment, and decided to change the subject.

"Why is there an armed guard at the entrance. Is there a war on?"

The porter shrugged expressively.

"There have been riots, Your Excellency. Bad elements near the docks have been causing trouble. But do not worry, you will be undisturbed here. Most of the hotel is occupied by gentlemen from the Syndicate. The guards have orders to shoot if there is any disturbance."

Mandrake bristled.

"Get out," he barked. "Orders to shoot! Lot of fascists!"

The startled porter backed away, clearly under the impression that Mandrake was mad.

When they were alone, Chip asked about the Syndicate.

"Heard of it, yes," said Mandrake. "International collection of businessmen. Started many years ago in mining all over the world. If Malik's in control they'll do anything, if there's a profit in it. I knew they'd bought up a lot of surplus armaments, guns, tanks, that sort of thing, after the last war. Started one or two small wars of their own in the Far East, and sold their wretched arms to both sides. Made a profit all right, caused a lot of misery too. Never realised that Malik was behind it."

"And what is Mr. Kreamer then?" asked Chip.

"One of the Syndicate's bullies, I suppose. Looks as though they're running the whole island. Bad state of affairs, very bad. My opinion . . ."

He was interrupted by a knock at the door. The porter ushered in a superior young man in a frock coat, who smiled and bowed formally. "Dr. Mandrake?" he inquired.

"I am he," admitted Mandrake grudgingly.

"Welcome to L'Île des Quatre Apôtres. My name is Raoul Vincent and I am private secretary to His Excellency the President. He has instructed me to wait on you and request that you be good enough to grant him an interview as soon as possible."

Mandrake stared.

"He requests me . . . Ha! That's good, I must say, young man. When is 'as soon as possible'? "

"Now, Dr. Mandrake," smiled Vincent. "A car awaits you."

"Very well, young man. Now it shall be. You must give me a few moments to make myself presentable. Chip, put your new clothes on. You are in no fit state for an official visit."

Vincent looked at Chip and raised his eyebrows.

"The invitation is for you alone, Dr. Mandrake."

"Never mind about that," snapped Mandrake. "I am responsible for this boy. Where I go, he goes. Don't fancy leaving him alone in this thieves' kitchen."

"I—I'll be all right," explained Chip, flushing.

"Do as you're told, Charles Wood," thundered Mandrake.

Chip hastily slipped into his bedroom and changed. He hardly recognised himself when he inspected the result in the mirror. Like most sandy-haired people he caught the sun easily and his face had turned a bright pink which contrasted with his new white clothes. His rather sharp features had filled out on the voyage and he was feeling fighting fit. He grinned encouragingly to himself and returned to the lounge.

Mandrake, who was still wearing his old clothes but had replaced the battered hat with a new Panama, inspected him approvingly. "Great improvement," he said briskly. "Now, Mr. Vincent, conduct us to your master."

Vincent shrugged sulkily, as though the whole business was beneath his dignity, and led the way to the entrance, where a gleaming American car was waiting with two motor-cycle escorts. It bore a green and white flag on the radiator and a gilt coat of arms above the front screen. It looked as big as the *Salamander* to Chip and, as it dipped down into the town, it had great difficulty in negotiating the narrow streets. To get to the President's palace on the hill of S. Jean they had to pass close to the docks again. From the increasing number of police, and the crowds of natives, it looked as though more trouble was brewing. But they were not interfered with and arrived at the gateway of the palace enclosure without incident. The official car was passed through without question by the sentries, who were dressed, like the first customs official, in olive green.

"I am afraid that from here it will be necessary to walk," said Vincent, breaking the frigid silence he had maintained since leaving the hotel. He was obviously put out by Mandrake's eccentric appearance and his insistence that Chip should accompany them.

They were just below the crest of the hill. A broad,

paved way ran up in steps across the terraces to the palace. As they had seen from the harbour, the hill was surrounded by a fortified wall. The lower slopes had been levelled to make space for barracks and parade grounds, but the mound before them had been laid out as an ornate park, with alcoves cut into the hillside and pavilions set among vivid shrubs and elaborate rock gardens.

"Must be smashing to have a garden like that, just for yourself," said Chip enviously.

"Ha! That's only part of it, boy," replied Mandrake. "Look at the way the alcoves and pavilions cover the approaches. A few guns in them and the palace would have been impregnable. Brilliant design. Don't approve of that sort of thing, but brilliant. Knew how to combine business with pleasure in the eighteenth century."

Ignoring Vincent's protests, he darted off along side paths on short tours of inspection.

"Strictly private to the President . . . no one, not even members of the Syndicate allowed . . ." fluttered the unhappy secretary, but Mandrake brushed him impatiently aside. He pointed to an inscription, partly covered by a vine.

" 'Le jardin de la dame blanche,' " he read. "Who was this lady, young man?"

Vincent shrugged sulkily.

"I don't know. The palace and gardens were the work of the first de Malpré. He is said to have made the gardens for the pleasure of his mother, but no one is sure. But, sir, please hurry. The President will not like waiting."

"No doubt, young man, no doubt," agreed Mandrake, who seemed to have recovered his good humour. "She must have been a lady of taste and discrimination and he a dutiful son. Excellent story, whether true or not."

Fussily, Vincent urged them back to the broad path,

but Mandrake still lagged behind, plunging into the shrub-
bery, examining the rocks and soil and finally, to Chip's
astonishment and Vincent's unconcealed disgust, slipped a
lump of stone into his pocket. This appeared to satisfy
him for he waved imperiously to Vincent and said:

"Lead us to him, young man. Lead us to him."

He hurried on up the hill so fast that neither Chip nor
the secretary could keep up with him.

The palace, like the hotel, was in the form of a hollow
square. Its forbidding exterior showed that it had been
built for defence, but, when they passed through the heavily
guarded entrance, it was as though they had stepped back
into an earlier and more gracious age. For, although Vincent
shepherded them along as rapidly as he could, Chip glimpsed
tapestried walls, gilded ceilings, plush hangings and crystal
chandeliers in the rooms they passed. A fort on the outside
and a palace within or, as Mandrake had said, business mixed
with pleasure.

Little sunlight penetrated the vast, deserted interior, and
a smell of decay hung in the echoing corridors, for the
tapestries were faded, the gilt tarnished, the hangings
threadbare and the crystal without lustre. It was a melancholy and, to Chip at any rate, rather ghostly place, which
gave him a nervous feeling of suffocation.

He was glad when Vincent ushered them through a
book-lined office on to a terrace overlooking the town
and harbour. The sun and fresh sea air were a relief after
the musty interior. "Your Excellency, Dr. Mandrake is
here," announced Vincent before withdrawing.

A big man in a green tunic got up from a reclining chair
and came impatiently towards them. His black hair had a
broad streak of grey in it, coming down in a peak on his
forehead. His swarthy features, which revealed his part-
native descent, were lined with fatigue and strain. Although

he had dignity and the air of one who expects obedience, he seemed tense and on edge.

His dark eyes ran over Chip casually, then fixed on Mandrake. His expression of surprise at Mandrake's unusual dress changed to amusement.

"It was good of you to come so quickly," he said. "Come and sit with me."

He stood at the balustrade looking across the bay to the yacht *Midas*, so far below that it looked like a toy. He did not speak again for so long that Mandrake cleared his throat irritably. Then he said:

"I deeply regret the death of Julius Schumann. He was a good man. I knew him many years ago, when we were students in Paris."

"Never told me of that, sir," replied Mandrake gruffly. The president smiled ironically.

"He wasn't proud of my friendship, Dr. Mandrake. He came to disapprove of me. You have seen the town of S. Jean. What is your opinion of it?"

Mandrake appeared disconcerted by the sudden change of subject.

"Ha!" he barked uncomfortably. "Is my opinion of importance?"

"It could be. It could be of the greatest importance."

Chip saw that Mandrake was at a loss for an answer. On the one hand it was against his nature to speak less than the truth, on the other he needed the President's good-will and did not want to offend him.

"Hungry children . . . ragged people, side by side with wealth . . . a disgrace . . . shameful!" replied Mandrake at length, and Chip had to stifle a nervous giggle at this less than tactful reply.

The President smiled briefly.

"Julius Schumann's sentiments precisely," he said.

"Unfortunately he held that I was entirely to blame. Do you know what the basic industry of the island is?"

"Copper," replied Mandrake, again rather put out by the abrupt change of subject. "Copper mining. Saw the workings when I was here years ago."

"Yes, of course you would have done. Let me tell you about them, they have to do with why I asked you to come. They were public property then, not producing much ore, but capable of extension. We needed better equipment and, most of all, a smelting plant. We sent the ore for smelting to the mainland. The Syndicate own mines and a plant there. They did it for us, and still do. We could not afford all these improvements, so I sold the mining rights for ten years to the Syndicate, in return for a fixed proportion of the profits and their agreement to erect a plant here, which would become our property at the end of that period. Was this not a reasonable thing to do?"

The President waited for Mandrake's reply and when none came, began distractedly pacing the terrace. The strain that had lined his face became apparent. When he continued he seemed almost to be talking to himself.

"I have asked myself this question many times. How could I have known into whose hands I was committing my people?"

With bitterness growing in his voice he explained how the Syndicate, who had promised so much, changed their tune. First the quality of the ore had been poorer than expected, then the cost of new equipment had been greater than expected, then the world price of copper had been lower than expected. With one excuse after another they had failed to carry out their part of the agreement. The smelting plant had not been built, wages had been pushed down until the natives were worse off than ever before. When they had rebelled and the President had sided with them, the

Syndicate had first threatened to leave the island, and then had brought in their own police to keep order.

"Why not let them go? Why not throw them out?" growled Mandrake, who was becoming steadily more angry.

The President shrugged impatiently. "He who rides a tiger finds it difficult to dismount," he quoted. "We would have starved, that is why. They would have taken all their equipment and refused to smelt our ore on the mainland. That was the crux of the matter, Dr. Mandrake. If they had built a plant here, I would have seized everything. But they were too cunning to have done that."

"A bad story," said Mandrake sombrely.

"That is not all of it. Now Josef Malik has arrived. I ask myself why? The Syndicate's agreement is shortly coming up for renewal. Now they want a larger share of the profits. Their excuse is that there have been several earth tremors which have damaged the workings and equipment. Is it for this that Malik has come?"

The President's dark features were suffused with rage he could contain no longer. His fist thudded on the stone coping until blood trickled unheeded from his knuckles. "It is not this he cares for. The surface workings are nearly exhausted, deep shafts must now be sunk. He could find richer pickings elsewhere."

"Flatly, sir, I don't understand all this," broke in Mandrake irritably. He was obviously not favourably impressed by the President's outburst. "Why else would Malik come if not for easy money?"

The interruption served to calm the President and give him time to control his anger. He stared at Mandrake searchingly before replying.

"You are not a man of affairs, Dr. Mandrake, otherwise you would know that the Syndicate are a power in the great money markets of the world. Their influence grows continually. Already they control the governments of some states in Africa and Asia. Small states, Dr. Mandrake, but with one thing in common, they each contain vital and rare materials which the great countries need . . ."

"That hardly applies to this island," said Mandrake. "Copper is found in many places . . ."

"Therefore Malik has not come about the copper," interrupted the President impatiently. "Then why has he come? For what, I ask myself? He commands the resources of his world-wide organisation from his yacht and yet he, the important Malik, comes himself. Why?" He stopped and waited for a reply but Mandrake remained silent.

"There is only one answer, Dr. Mandrake—your friend, Julius Schumann. He was a great man, a great scientist, with an international reputation for his work in atomic research. There is a rumour that he has made an important discovery. That apparently is enough to tempt Malik to come here. But why? He arrives. Six days later Schumann is dead; murdered."

"Why are you telling me all this, sir?" demanded Mandrake suddenly. "I know nothing of these matters. What bearing do they have on Julius Schumann's death?"

The President looked at him calculatingly before replying: "Schumann discovered something on the island. The Syndicate were trying to find out what it was, when they killed him. I cannot prove that, but I know. What was it he discovered, Dr. Mandrake?"

Mandrake's expression of astonishment was almost comical.

"Upon my soul! How should I know? I was not here." His sincerity was so plain that the President turned away impatiently.

"He wrote to you for equipment, which you have brought. What is it for? You must know that."

Mandrake shook his head.

"I am an archæologist, he was a physicist. I know very little of his work and nothing of his discovery."

The President stared at him coldly.

"I mean to have his discovery, Dr. Mandrake. If it is valuable, and it must be, I shall throw the Syndicate out, open new workings and build a plant myself. If Malik finds it, he will not disclose it until after a new agreement is signed. We shall be at the Syndicate's mercy for another ten years on worse terms than ever. Also, if the discovery is dangerous, what will it mean in the hands of a world-wide organisation that is nothing but a conspiracy for power? It is not acceptable!"

Mandrake nodded.

"I understand," he said curtly. "But I know nothing."

Chip saw the distrust on his face and so, too, did the President, for his manner became more distant. He rang a bell summoning Vincent.

"If you find any clue, Dr. Mandrake, when you go into the interior, you are to let me know at once. Do not speak to anyone of what I have told you."

He stood up abruptly to show that, as far as he was concerned, the rather profitless interview was over.

Mandrake was silent and preoccupied as they walked down the hill to the car. Chip stumbled after him, his eyes drawn irresistibly to the *Midas* in the bay. He could imagine her, immaculate and sinister, gliding into ports and harbours in Africa and the East, carrying the inscrutable Malik in search of hidden wealth. He could imagine too the wireless messages flashing between the yacht and the Syndicate's agents in Europe and America bearing information and instructions, summoning men like Kreamer, blocking resistence to the schemes which would rob backward countries, struggling for existence, of their resources and hopes for the future. His sun-scorched face became even redder at the unfairness of it. It was Silverman all over again, but Silverman on a grand, international scale.

He cannoned into Vincent who had halted beside the car. The secretary, still silent and disapproving, bowed his farewell to Mandrake and ignored Chip. But Chip was too wrapped up in his own angry thoughts to notice. Once in the car, he looked at Mandrake out of the corner of his eyes, but seeing the doctor's preoccupied expression, settled back without speaking to puzzle over the secret that had apparently died with Julius Schumann.

They ran downhill towards the docks, before the long ascent back to the hotel. There seemed to be even more people in the streets than there had been earlier, and the driver had difficulty in getting through. He kept his finger continually on the horn to clear a passage.

Suddenly they came to such an abrupt stop that Chip was flung violently forward. He stared over the driver's shoulder. The narrow street ahead was completely blocked with chanting people who were marching in procession. Almost immediately the car was surrounded.

"What is it, driver?" rapped Mandrake irritably. "Go on, go on, man. Sound your horn, do something!"

"It is a procession, your excellency," stammered the driver. "They are fobidden by law, but they go on all the time."

"Nothing to do with us, drive on!"

But it was easier said than done. The press about the car was jammed tight.

Chip braced himself, determined not to show that he was scared, but the dark, glowering faces pressed against the windows were enough to frighten anyone, they were so threatening and full of hatred. The noise was deafening as the top and sides of the car were thumped with fists and sticks. Mandrake shouted angrily, but Chip could not hear what he was saying. One native, more daring than the rest, scrambled on to the bonnet and, with a savage jerk, wrenched away the President's coat of arms and tossed it back into the crowd. It was like a signal releasing a storm of violence. The uproar turned again into a chant as the crowd started rocking the heavy vehicle, working up enough momentum to turn it over.

The panic-stricken driver forced open his door to get away, but there was no chance. Clutching hands reached in to grab him and he disappeared screaming under a storm of blows.

Chip flung his arms up to protect his face from flying glass as the car reared up on one side, hesitated, and crashed over.

He found himself spread-eagled on top of Mandrake, who struggled furiously to get free.

"Keep down, boy," came Mandrake's muffled voice. "If they get us out of here they'll kill us. Keep down."

Chip crouched down groping for something to use as a weapon. If the rioters were determined to get them out of the wrecked car, he was equally determined to make a fight of it. After the initial shock he felt his temper rising. An ominous silence fell outside, as though the crowd were shocked by what they had done.

"May be the police," muttered Mandrake. "They must know what's going on by this time."

Chip sniffed.

"There's something burning," he said suddenly. "They're setting fire to the car!"

Mandrake gripped his arm urgently.

"We must risk the crowd then. Up on my shoulders—don't argue!"

But before Chip could move, someone bounded up on

the side of the car and a deep-throated voice boomed at the crowd, but what it said was lost in a storm of jeers and cat-calls. The shattered window above them darkened as a massive black hand was thrust down through the opening.

"You do like I say, quick," growled the deep voice. "Give me your hand. Don't you be afraid."

Chip grabbed the outstretched hand. His shoulder was nearly dislocated as he was hauled up through the shattered window and dumped unceremoniously into the road. Mandrake followed a minute later.

The crowd still surrounded them, but were pressing back away from the towering figure standing on the side of the upturned car. Although some of them shouted threateningly, they did so half-heartedly. When Chip looked up, he understood why, for the man on the car was a magnificent full-blooded negro. He must have been nearly seven feet in height, and perfectly proportioned. In spite of his ragged singlet and shorts he was a dominating figure.

His great voice rang out over the murmuring of the crowd: "Get about your business, you ignorant natives. You fight when I tell you to fight. You go home when I tell you to go home. These men are my prisoners. I'll deal with them as I decide. You get along before the black trousers come."

"Watch out, King," piped a boy in the crowd. "The car's burning. It's on fire."

The negro glanced down to the back of the car, leapt clear, and grabbing Chip and Mandrake, bundled them through the crowd.

"Get back," he roared. "Less you want to get fried. Back, the lot of you."

The warning came none too soon, for a bundle of smouldering rags, which had been thrust into the boot, burst into flames. An instant later the tank exploded like a bomb, filling the air with flying metal and flaming petrol.

The crowd took to its heels and melted away. Above the racket Chip heard police sirens and, in the distance, shots being fired.

"You come," growled the negro. "Stupid natives. They don't know nothing."

He shoved Mandrake and Chip up a side street into a maze of alleys. Mandrake did not relish this treatment and, having recovered his breath, refused to go any farther.

"Obliged to you for getting us out of a nasty predicament," he gasped. "But I demand to know where you are taking us. Refuse to go another step until I know."

The negro paused to look down at him.

"Now don't you ask me no questions, Dr. Mandrake. Just you come. No one's going to harm you, sir. Leastways, not while you're with me. I'm taking you to see my chief, Richard Liberté, that's all I'll say."

Mandrake was obviously taken aback that the negro knew his name. He glanced around at the unsavoury shacks through which the alleys ran.

"Very well," he agreed grudgingly. "But there's no need to hold on to me like that. Take your hands off me."

The negro's face split into a brilliant grin.

"If you say so, Dr. Mandrake, sir," he chuckled. "But don't you try to run off, now."

He led the way across an empty plot of waste land, down a flight of brick steps, to a battered door in the basement of a ruined building. He pounded on the door, and shouted for it to be opened. Bolts were drawn inside, and a chain unloosed. They were hustled through into semi-darkness beyond.

CHAPTER SIX

WITH THE REVOLUTIONARIES

When his eyes became accustomed to the gloom, Chip saw that they were in a low-beamed cellar, piled high with rubbish, but it was too dark to see anything clearly.

"Go right ahead, fellers," rumbled the negro, bent almost double in the confined space.

He pushed them on towards the rear of the building. They stumbled down another short flight of steps and came to a second door. Again there was the sound of bolts and a chain and, as the door swung back, a flood of light came out to greet them. A native boy stood holding the door open for them. Chip saw that they were in the boiler room of a wrecked building. It must have been a massive place at one time, for there was a giant bank of dead furnaces, streaked with rust, along one wall.

But what caught his eye at once, was a group of natives, squatting under a naked light bulb around a writing desk in the centre of the room. They had been listening attentively to a young man, who was showing them a rifle. He stopped as they entered, and looked round.

"I got them, chief," called the negro. "Dr. Mandrake and this boy here. Like you said."

The young man came across. He was dressed in khaki shirt and shorts and had two revolvers strapped to his waist. For a moment he reminded Chip of the President. He had the same dark skin and cast of features, his hair came down in the same peak on his forehead, but there the resemblance ended, for he had a wispy beard and his expression was anything but courteous. He stared at Mandrake venomously.

"Welcome to the headquarters of the Revolutionary Freedom Party, Dr. Mandrake," he said in an intense, high-pitched voice. "Not as comfortable as your hotel, perhaps, but you see we are not friends of the President or Josef Malik's Syndicate. We are just the people of this island. I am Richard Liberté, the leader of the party."

His offensive manner was too much for Mandrake, who had been muttering angrily to himself ever since they had entered the building.

"Don't know who you are, neither do I care," he barked. "But I insist that you release us immediately. I have no business with you . . ."

"But you had business with the Syndicate and the President," cut in Liberté. "Now we have business with you."

"State it, then," snapped Mandrake.

"I want to know what it was that made it necessary for your friends in the Syndicate to murder Professor Schumann."

"Friends!" exploded Mandrake. "How dare you. Impudent young ruffian. Don't know what Julius Schumann discovered, and if I did, I would not tell you, nor would I tell the President, nor Malik and his Syndicate."

He was so enraged that he thrust his bristling beard into Liberté's face. Apparently the negro thought that worse would follow, for he stretched out a restraining hand. As at the palace, Mandrake's sincerity was obvious. The young revolutionary was disconcerted. He glanced at the expectant faces of the squatting natives. Clearly they had understood nothing of this exchange. He dismissed them curtly and waited until they had filed from the room.

"Bolt the door, King," he called to the negro, and when this was done: "Now, Dr. Mandrake. Perhaps you will explain."

"What is there for me to explain?" demanded Mandrake. "If anyone should explain, it is you. I came here to see my friend, Julius Schumann. I find that he has been brutally murdered. Everyone thinks I know why. I don't. But I promise you I mean to find out."

Liberté's doubtful expression wavered and gave way to one of dejection and gloom. He sighed dispiritedly and perched himself on the edge of the desk.

"I thought you would be able to help us. Professor Schumann was our friend. If he was murdered by the Syndicate, it must have been because he had discovered something of value to the people. The fact that Josef Malik is now here means that the discovery is at least worth stealing. We are the party of the people." He began to recover his spirits, and as he spoke about the Party and the people, he sounded to Chip as though he were addressing a public meeting. "We shall free the island of the slavery, the servitude. The revolution will destroy the Dictator and the hold of the Syndicate. The day of the government of the people by the . . ."

"Yes, yes," snapped Mandrake acidly. "No doubt this will be a splendid thing, although if by the people you mean the rabble who nearly murdered us in the street just now, I hope I am not here to see it. However, all beside the point. I shall be obliged if you will tell your assistant here to show us the way back to our hotel."

The negro grinned, his teeth gleaming even in the dim light.

"What you say, chief?" he demanded. "Shall I rough this Mandrake up some?"

Liberté ignored the interruption. His thin cheeks flushed angrily. "This is not a joke, Dr. Mandrake. When you have been here longer you will understand what conditions the people have to endure. The Syndicate is merciless and the

President is useless. He has sold himself. I am their only hope. Professor Schumann did not sneer at us. We need *help*, not ridicule. Somewhere on the island there is hope for us. We don't know what or where. All we know is that Malik is here to steal it from us."

Mandrake sank wearily into the chair behind the desk and looked at him quizzically.

"Forgive me, but this has been a trying day. I *have* already seen the conditions here. Disgusting! Like to help you. No good will come of riots. The natives are like sheep against armed police. You should not encourage them."

"I do not encourage them," shouted Liberté, looking at the negro and shaking his fist. "This was your fault, King. I told you your processions would lead to trouble. We are not yet ready."

The negro hung his head, like a little boy.

"Sorry, chief," he mumbled uncomfortably.

"I don't know what the President told you," went on Liberté angrily. "But I guess he did not tell you that three months ago the Syndicate were preparing to leave the island when their present agreement ran out. If they stayed they would need new workings because the present ones are nearly finished. They are not prepared to spend money to help the island. They can make easier profits elsewhere. Then the rumour started that Professor Schumann had made a great discovery. At first I believed it was another rich deposit of copper that they could mine easily. Now that Malik has come I am not sure it is just copper. But it was when this rumour began that the Syndicate started bringing in foreigners as their private police."

"Don't understand why," interrupted Mandrake, who had been listening attentively. "They were already established here and you say the President did not want them to go."

Liberté shrugged expressively.

"He is weak and prefers what they offer, rather than facing, with courage, the difficulties there would be if they went. But, of course, if Professor Schumann had discovered a new and easily worked deposit the President would not renew the agreement. He is not a bad man, just weak."

"Weak," echoed Mandrake with a faint smile. "But if there was no valuable secret and the Syndicate left the island, what then? You would all starve. Is that right?"

"We could go back to farming the land," replied Liberté stiffly. "And we should at least be free."

Mandrake sat lost in thought while Chip, who had been biting his fingers with excitement, gave voice to the question that had been bothering him.

"I still do not understand why the Syndicate murdered Professor Schumann if they wanted his secret."

Liberté glanced at him for the first time, smiling faintly at the eager enthusiasm on his face:

"He lived in an old fort in the interior near the mines. They kidnapped him and he was shot trying to escape. This was a mistake, I believe."

This rang a bell for Chip. He recalled Kreamer's anger at receiving the wireless message on the *Salamander*. He had said something to Petit about a disastrous mistake. He must have been referring to the murder. In fact, had not Mandrake said so at the time?

"I think it's true, Dr. Mandrake," he blurted out. Now he had heard the whole story he was completely on the young revolutionary's side and he wanted to persuade Mandrake to help. "Can't we do something?"

He was rewarded by a broad grin from King, and an approving glance from Liberté.

"Yes, sir," said the negro. "Amen to that."

"What's your part in this?" snapped Mandrake at King. "Where are you from?"

The negro was taken aback at the suspicious tone.

"Me, sir? I'm British. Born in Jamaica. I worked for ten-twelve years in America, but I'm British. Napoleon's my name. King Napoleon, that's me, sir."

Mandrake's face relaxed.

"Fine old English name, that," he said gravely.

"Yes, sir," beamed King. "Thank you, sir."

Mandrake seemed reassured. He stood up and put his hand on Liberté's shoulder.

"Can't promise to help. But, if I find I can, I will. Must give me your word, Richard Liberté, that you will stop your friends from rioting in the streets."

Liberté glanced immediately at King, who hung his head again.

"I will try, Dr. Mandrake, but it is difficult, you know. They feel the need of revolution to cast off their chains with violence, to cleanse . . ."

"Where did you learn to talk like that?" interrupted Mandrake, becoming irritable again.

Liberté flushed.

"In Paris. I was at the university there."

"Can well imagine it," said Mandrake acidly. "Now, let our friend Napoleon here conduct Charles Wood and myself back to our hotel. After the funeral of my poor friend, I shall go into the interior. One of the purposes of my visit, to continue work on the city of the Gardiens. Have permission to do so. Good excuse to visit the house of Julius Schumann and see what I can discover there. Remember, in the meanwhile, no violence."

"I shall try," said Liberté. "You have my word."

He gave instructions to King, who conducted them from the cellar back into the open air and through the tangle of alleyways. Dark faces peered suspiciously at them as they passed. Chip was glad enough of King's company and followed closely on the negro's heels. He could feel the hostile eyes almost boring into his back and could guess what would have happened to Mandrake and himself, had they been alone.

"He's a good boy, that Richard," said King over his shoulder. "Only trouble, he's too soft on that President. Lots of our boys want to shoot him. But young Richard won't let them, no sir. Trains them to use guns, then won't let them use them. It's against nature, Dr. Mandrake, sir. A man's got to fight."

Mandrake grunted, but made no reply.

They came to a main thoroughfare and King halted. The street was quiet enough, but in the distance the sound of shooting showed that there was still trouble near the docks.

"You'll be all right here, Dr. Mandrake. You go down to that corner there and you'll find a taxi outside the bank. I'd better not come no farther, you see. Don't want no fighting, like you said, Dr. Mandrake." He grinned broadly and winked at Chip. "No, sir, but it's against nature."

"It's important," said Mandrake solemnly. "Remember. Otherwise you'll be in trouble, and your friends too."

King nodded.

"That's what they told me in America, sir. 'We don't want no fighting here, boy,' they said, then they sent me back to Jamaica."

"Why didn't you stay there?"

"They don't like fighting there, neither, sir. So I came here. Looked like trouble, so I came."

"Shows a fine spirit," said Mandrake with a reluctant smile. "Just remember what I said."

The massive negro stood at the end of the alley and watched them cross to the bank. The last they saw of him was a cheery wave and shining smile. He dodged out of sight as an armoured car roared by on its way to the docks.

"Child of nature, that," muttered Mandrake with a twinkle in his eyes. "The noble savage, eh, Chip?"

But in spite of his apparent good humour, he quickly fell silent again when they were in the taxi making for their hotel. But Chip was too excited to keep quiet.

"What do you think, Dr. Mandrake?" he asked eagerly. "Are we going to help them?"

"Help them?" echoed Mandrake. "Don't know that we're in a position to help anyone. First the President, then this Richard Liberté think that I can discover what Julius Schumann's secret was, just like that. They must have tried already, and the Syndicate too, and failed. Why should I succeed?"

"Perhaps because you're a scientist, like him?" suggested Chip helpfully.

"Well, I'm not," snapped Mandrake. "I'm an archæologist, not a physicist. Told you that already. Stop biting your fingers. It annoys me."

"But if it's a deposit of copper, don't you know about rocks and things," persisted Chip.

Mandrake frowned and pulled out the piece of stone he had picked up in the palace grounds. He stared at it with a puzzled expression before returning it to his pocket.

"Know something of geology," he replied absently, "but that's not the answer to this problem, Chip. The equipment I've brought for Julius Schumann is nothing to do with copper or any other metal."

"What's it for, then?"

"Examining very highly radioactive material."

"You mean things like . . . like uranium?" asked Chip excitedly.

He had read in the papers about strikes of uranium and

had some idea of how valuable they were as a source of atomic power. If Professor Schumann had discovered uranium, it would explain Malik's interest. It would also solve the island's problems, provided it did not fall into the Syndicate's hands.

Mandrake shook his head.

"No, no. Nothing like that. This is more the sort of equipment used in laboratories for examining processed radioactive substances, not crude ores. Julius certainly had no equipment for processing such material. Cost a fortune and require an experienced staff. Out of the question. This is a strange island, full of secrets: Xarpata, his two wives, and now the discovery of poor Julius."

Chip tried to hide his disappointment. He wondered whether there was any link between Xarpata and Schumann's secret, but before he could think up any ideas the taxi had pulled into the driveway of the hotel. "Not a word about this," said Mandrake. "Never know who may overhear in this place. Be glad to leave it."

There was now half a dozen or so black-uniformed guards in the entrance, but they were minding their own business and appeared to be a precaution against any rioters who might take it into their heads to attack the hotel.

The clerk looked at Mandrake curiously when asked for the key, and seemed about to speak, but apparently thought better of it.

"I shall be glad of the opportunity to compose myself," said Mandrake rather wearily as they mounted the stairs. "If to-day is a sample of what we must expect, our stay on the island of the Four Apostles will prove exhausting."

Chip followed him into their private lounge. The blinds had been drawn against the heat and the room was cool and shady. All the same he was intent on getting under a shower as quickly as he could. The oppressive heat outside had made his clothes cling uncomfortably to him. He promised himself that just for a few moments he would forget Malik, the Syndicate, the President, the riots, the lot, under a spray of cold, refreshing water.

A bulky, familiar figure rose from an easy-chair by the balcony window, and advanced towards them.

"Dr. Mandrake," said Jason Kreamer, his pale eyes gleaming in the half light. "You must forgive this intrusion, but I find that it is I who need help, your help. Herr Malik has ordered me to make this request."

CHAPTER SEVEN

PRISONER OF THE SYNDICATE

MANDRAKE made a visible effort to hide his irritation at Kreamer's unexpected visit. Brusquely he waved Kreamer to be seated, but the German shook his head.

"I shall not disturb you for long. I know that you have had a busy time since you landed." He paused just long enough to let them wonder how much he did know. "I shall come straight to the point. I know also that you have not bound yourself to tell the President what you may discover of Schumann's work. I trust you have given no such undertaking to our young revolutionary friend, either. Herr Malik's request is this, that should you, while you are on the island, find what Schumann discovered, you will at once let me know."

Mandrake stared at him as though he could not believe his ears.

"You see," continued Kreamer imperturbably, "We are quite sure that this is nothing so simple as a new copper deposit. Our geologists have already examined every square foot of the northern half of the island, except perhaps under the President's palace." He laughed softly at his own joke. "They would have discovered such a thing long ago. Copper in the forests south of the island would hardly be worth the expense of mining. There are no roads, railways, or harbours there, besides which, as you know, the forests are still inhabited by the Gardiens—a savage and unreliable tribe. It would be impossible to get any workers. No, no. I fancy that Schumann's discovery was much more important than copper. My Syndicate intend to have it, Dr. Mandrake. I will not insult you by offering you money, but the Syndicate would express their appreciation in any way you choose."

"You should not have had Julius Schumann murdered," roared Mandrake, suddenly recovering his tongue. "You could then have asked him."

Kreamer sighed.

"Would it make you feel any better, Dr. Mandrake, to know that my first action on arriving here was to have the man responsible for that most regrettable accident shot?"

Chip felt a chill pass through the room. Kreamer spoke about having people shot as though it were of no more consequence than swatting flies. Mandrake's uncertain control over his temper finally gave way. Shaking with rage, he thrust his beard down towards Kreamer's face.

"Under no circumstances will I help you," he shouted. "Neither Malik nor his murderous Syndicate will lay one finger on any discovery of Julius Schumann while I have a breath in my body. Now get out of here Kreamer, before I throw you out. Old man I may be, but throw you out I will."

Kreamer seemed quite unmoved.

"You must admit, Dr. Mandrake," he said patiently, "I have tried to do this quietly and without offence. Now I have no choice. Louis!" The lattice blind over the balcony door was pushed aside to reveal Petit. He stood there, more grotesque then ever, his eyes flickering from Mandrake to Chip and then to Kreamer.

"Take the boy, Louis," said Kreamer. "Be careful, he is a slippery little customer."

There had been something nightmarish about a friendly Kreamer, and in a way Chip felt relieved that the German was coming into the open. All the same his heart thudded painfully and his first instinct was to run, but he knew he dared not turn his back. He chewed his lip, steeling himself to make a fight of it as the small man sidled across the room.

"Leave the boy alone," roared Mandrake. "I am responsible for his safety."

Kreamer stepped back and produced an automatic.

"Exactly, Dr. Mandrake, so you are. If we take him with us he will be the guarantee of your co-operation."

Mandrake glared at him balefully, for once at a loss for a reply. Chip took his eyes from Petit for an instant to glance at Kreamer. It was enough. With one sudden movement Petit was behind him, twisting his right arm up in a half-nelson. Something pricked viciously in his back.

"Don't struggle, he has a knife," cried Mandrake desperately. Chip gritted his teeth. There was nothing much else he could do.

"*Allez-y,*" hissed Petit, urging him on to the balcony. In the courtyard below a closed truck was waiting. A black-uniformed driver stood beside it, looking up at them.

"Jump," snarled Petit, pushing Chip to the balustrade. Chip swung his leg over the rail and let himself go. He landed in a bed of shrubs. Two gaily-coloured birds rose screaming about his head and made off across the roofs. Before he could recover his balance the driver was on him and had bundled him into the back of the truck. A few minutes later Petit scrambled in beside him and the door was slammed and locked.

Petit deliberately slid his knife into a sheath strapped to his forearm, where it was ready for instant action, and settled himself on a spare wheel. He did not take his narrow eyes off Chip for an instant.

They waited for Kreamer, who was not apparently prepared to leap from the balcony. Chip watched him through the ventilator in the side of the truck as he came across the courtyard. He was quite at ease, as though kidnapping was all part of the day's work to him. He climbed in beside the driver and the truck pulled away smartly.

Once clear of the hotel, it turned south and sped along a straight, well-surfaced road out of the built-up area. Chip tried to remember the map of the island. As far as he could tell, they were heading for the range of hills across the waist of the island in which the copper mines were located. His guess was confirmed a little later when they dropped down into a valley beside a river. On the farther bank, he could see the narrow-gauge mineral railway that linked the mines with the port of S. Jean.

They soon ran on to a broad, featureless plateau, across which the river flowed sluggishly in great meanders. There was no other traffic and the truck picked up speed, trailing clouds of dust behind it.

On either side the land was cultivated, but, although Chip knew little enough about farming, he could recognise in the broken fences and overgrown hedges the same signs of depression and neglect he had seen in S. Jean. No one seemed to be working in the fields, which were mostly unkempt and full of weeds. The villages they passed through were the same, broken down and ramshackle. Groups of peasants stood by the road, watching impassively as the truck roared through. There were few men to be seen, mostly there were only women and small children.

Chip glanced hopefully across at Petit who seemed to have been overcome by the heat and on the point of dropping off to sleep. Petit stirred and let his knife slide from its sheath to his skinny hand. He bared his teeth as though he had read Chip's thoughts.

Gradually the airless heat in the closed van and the monotonous drumming of the tyres overcame Chip's own watchfulness and his head began to swim. How long he was like that, between sleeping and waking, he did not know. It seemed like hours before he was aroused, as a sharp turn in the road sent him sprawling.

The truck ran on to a rough surface and jerked to a halt. When the door was flung open, Chip was dragged out by the driver into the blinding sunlight. Petit stretched himself and followed stiffly.

Above them loomed the hills of the Copper Belt, scarred by the terraces of old surface workings. Giant earth-moving machines crawled across the slopes, gouging out the hillside in broad swathes, which stretched as far as the eye could see. At intervals along the workings, crushing plants churned out ore into endless conveyor belts running down to the railway.

He was not left for long to take in the ugly scene, for Kreamer appeared round the side of the truck, looking hot and dishevelled, his usually immaculate suit crumpled from the uncomfortable journey.

"Why do you wait, Petit? You know what to do with the boy," he snapped. "Take the driver with you. Report back to me at the manager's office." He stared coldly at Chip's sullen face. "Try to get away and the dogs will be put on to you."

The driver led Chip off along a dirt road, while Petit trailed behind, still rubbing the cramp out of his stiffened muscles and muttering bitterly to himself.

The road curved sharply after a hundred yards or so and Chip saw before him a hutted camp huddled in a fold in the hillside. It was surrounded by a high barbed-wire fence patrolled by Syndicate police. When he saw them he understood Kreamer's parting threat, for each of the black-uniformed figures was accompanied by a mastiff on a short lead.

The armed guard on the gates glanced curiously at Chip as he let them through. Over the gates, worked in metal, was the mailed fist symbol of the Syndicate. It was a constant reminder of the threatening power it represented.

The camp was laid out with barrack-like sleeping quarters fronting along concrete paths and grouped around large service buildings. Although they were well kept, the whole place had the bleak look of a prison about it. Apart from occasional guards it appeared completely deserted.

Neither the driver nor Petit spoke as they trudged along. They knew where they were going and did not need to discuss it. They halted beside a guard hut and Petit went in. He reappeared with a guard carrying a bunch of keys and a torch. The guard looked at Chip as questioningly as the man on the gate had done, but, when Petit snapped at him in rapid French, he shrugged his shoulders and led the way towards the opening of an underground shaft in the face of the hill. He unlocked a sheet steel door set in concrete and pulled it back, exposing a pitch-black opening from which came a babel of voices and a wave of stale air, heavy with the smell of unwashed bodies. He jerked his head to Chip and went inside, switching on his torch as he did so.

"*Taisez-vous!*" he yelled, and the noise died down. There were a few whispers, then silence. He played the beam along a line of steel doors, revealing brown faces staring through barred openings. Chip realised that he was in an abandoned mine shaft, which had been converted into a prison. The guard stalked along, jangling his keys and flashing his torch into the cells. He must have examined fifty or sixty before finding one that was unoccupied. He unlocked the door and nodded to the driver, who sent Chip sprawling inside. The door clanged shut. Chip scrambled to his feet to be confronted with Petit's face grinning spite-fully at him through the opening.

"Sit there and hope your friend Mandrake is a reasonable man," hissed Petit. "Otherwise you will just sit there."

He snickered as though the idea pleased him and then disappeared. Chip heard footsteps receding along the shaft. The torchlight grew dimmer until it finally vanished, leaving him in complete darkness and silence.

He had a horror of being shut in confined spaces and felt panic rising and choking him. He bit his fingers desperately to stop himself shouting after Petit, begging to be let out. Cold perspiration broke out on his forehead and ran down his cheeks. Then, gradually, his natural obstinacy came to his aid as it always did to prevent him giving way to panic.

Fortunately the silence did not last, for soon after the outer door of the shaft thudded to, the other prisoners started whispering, then chattering, and finally shouting, until the noise was deafening. All the same it was several minutes before he could muster up enough courage to move. His predicament seemed quite hopeless. He did not doubt that Mandrake would already be doing everything possible to set him free. But what was there he could do? The President was not likely to help, even if he could. He had his own game to play with Malik and the Syndicate. Richard Liberté had his hands full controlling his followers and keeping them out of trouble. The only certain way was for Mandrake to help the Syndicate in finding Schu-mann's discovery, and that Chip set his mind resolutely against. He could not bear the thought that Mandrake might do that on his account, the idea of it made him clench his fists with anger, the same anger that had made him resist the threats of Silverman. He pictured the Syndicate as consisting of Maliks and Silvermans, with Kreamers and

Petits, dozens of them, in attendance. Their faces seemed to float in the darkness in front of him, the lined, blank face and dead eyes of Malik, the white fleshy face of Silverman, the . . .

He pulled himself up with a jerk. There was only one answer. He would have to break out of the prison and get back to Mandrake on his own. He was determined not to be the cause of Malik getting his hands on Julius Schumann's discovery and it was up to him.

Having made up his mind he felt better, keyed up for action. He stood listening to the row the other prisoners were making, wondering what his first move should be. In the darkness it was difficult to make out what the chances were of getting out of the cell. He ran his hands over the door. It was sheet-steel and there was no hope there. The wall on either side of it was concrete and would have taken a pneumatic drill to penetrate. He groped his way across to a side wall. It seemed to be made of timber, which was more promising, but hope quickly faded for the timber felt tough and solid, probably old supports from the workings.

Baffled, he tried the floor with his heel. It was the natural earth floor of the shaft and had no hard surface. He dropped to his knees and dug his fingers into the soil. With persistence and any luck he would be able to burrow underneath the timber wall into the next cell. What good that would do he was not sure, since all the cells were behind the steel and concrete side of the shaft, which would have to be breached before there was any real chance of freedom, but it was a start and better than doing nothing.

Still on his knees, he cast around for something, anything, to dig with. Then he froze in his tracks, his scalp tingling, for as he leaned forward, two hands came up out of the darkness and clutched at his face.

He was sure the cell had been empty when he had been thrown into it. Now he was no longer alone.

"Sir! sir!" A muffled voice came from almost beneath his feet. "Help me. Take my hands. I must talk with you."

"Who are you?" began Chip, then realised that it did not matter. Anyone in prison here was almost certainly a friend, whether they knew it yet or not. He discovered that the outstretched hands were sticking up from a narrow hole in the floor. The other prisoners apparently had not been wasting their time either. He grasped the hands and heaved. There was a brief struggle, a wail of pain, and the owner of the hands squirmed out of the hole.

"Are you all right?" cried Chip anxiously.

"Yis, I think," moaned the voice unhappily. "I am now quite well, sir. I believe so."

"Who are you? Who are all these prisoners?"

"Yis, yis. So many questions you ask. First you tell me who you are, and for what reason you have joined us."

Chip explained briefly who he was and what had happened, while his new companion listened silently, except for an exclamation when Mandrake's name was mentioned.

"I'd do anything to stop Dr. Mandrake being forced to help Malik's Syndicate, and that's why I must get away from here," finished up Chip grimly. "Can you help me? I'm sorry, but I don't know who you are or how you know about Dr. Mandrake."

"Ah, yis, yis. My name is Mr. Gopal. You see, I was respected Professor Schumann's servant. I was with him many, many years, ever since he visited Calcutta before the war. I am from Calcutta, you see. When the respected Professor was murdered, I was thrown into this place by evil men. I knew I must speak with you when I saw the guards bring you. Only a glimpse I had, in the light of their torches. But any European imprisoned by the evil men must be a friend. This I know. Professor Schumann told me that Dr. Mandrake was coming, but of his arrival, of course, I did not know."

"It's a bit of luck that you're in the next cell," said Chip.

"No, no, not in next cell. They are all connected by tunnels the prisoners have made."

"All?" echoed Chip.

"Yis," said Mr. Gopal sadly. "But this is no use. The end walls of the end cells are concrete. The front wall, too. It is not possible to get out, only from one cell to another. Very sorry for this."

"Would the other prisoners help us escape?" asked Chip, searching for any ray of hope. "Who are they, anyway? Why are they in here?"

"Just natives who did not want to work here any longer," replied Mr. Gopal. "You see, the Syndicate offered high wages, most attractive, to bring them here. They come very happy. But, once arrived, they find they have to pay the Syndicate for their food, their tools, for insurance. Very high prices. If they make mistake, break rules, there are many, many rules, they are fined. So, to finish, they are working for nothing. They owe the Syndicate money. They are slaves, sir. They want to go home, but the Syndicate say, 'No, you sign contract, you owe money. You stay.' If they try to escape they are put in here."

It sounded true to the Syndicate's form. This was the other side of the luxurious yacht in the bay of S. Jean. This was the price to be paid for Malik's easy profits and greed for power. Chip grimaced disgustedly.

"Don't worry, Mr. Gopal," he said. "We'll get out. But you still haven't told me. Will the other prisoners help us?"

Mr. Gopal clicked doubtfully.

"Much as they hate the Syndicate, they are not really

fierce people, Mr. Wood. At least, not until they have a leader. Not like the Gardiens, who have a bad name for being fierce."

"None of these people are Gardiens then?"

"No, no, Mr. Wood. These people all come from the South American mainland, many generations ago, to work in the mines and the fields. The Gardiens are too proud to work for others. They were driven into the forests in the south of the island, beyond the Copper Belt. They were terrible in war, but now they are few and give no trouble unless they are disturbed. Professor Schumann told me this. He knew them well. He was their friend. They guard the mountain of their god Xarpata, who hides from his two wives, and keep to themselves."

"Pity we haven't got a few of them with us now," said Chip. "We could do with a few people who are terrible in war."

"Ay, ay, ay," said Mr. Gopal sadly. "Indeed that is so."

They squatted side by side in the darkness while Chip racked his brains for an idea, but short of burrowing a tunnel right out of the hill, there seemed to be no way open.

"Without tools, Mr. Wood? Not possible. And even if we could, we should still need to get out of the camp. It is guarded by terrible dogs." Mr. Gopal shuddered at the thought of them.

After more thought, Chip saw a gleam of hope.

"What happens when the guards bring food, Mr. Gopal?"

"What happens? Nothing happens. Two guards bring in containers and serve tins of horrible food and water, once a day."

"When?"

"In the evening, after the workers are back in camp. It is

such a bad diet, Mr. Wood. No fresh vegetables. No fruit. No protein. No vitamins. Ay, ay."

"Do the guards unlock the doors?"

"No, they pass the tins through the bars. They are very rude if you do not take your tin quickly. They throw the food on the floor and you get nothing."

Chip thought hard. Then he gripped Mr. Gopal's shoulder. It was a very thin and bony shoulder.

"I've got it," he exclaimed. "But you and the other prisoners will have to help."

"I trust it is not too violent," said Mr. Gopal. "I am not a violent man. I have always believed in peaceful resistance to force, Mr. Wood."

"And look where it's got you," interrupted Chip impatiently. Somehow he felt all the braver for Mr. Gopal's nervousness.

"In here, yis," admitted Mr. Gopal unhappily. "Ay, ay."

"This is what we'll do. I want you to tell the others to crawl through their tunnels into the cells farthest from the shaft entrance, so that several of the cells near the entrance will be empty. That will get the guards worried. We shall be in the first cell they see with anyone in it."

"They will not be pleased with us," murmured Mr. Gopal. "I feel sure they will not."

"I shall be lying on the floor, as though I am dead or something. You will hide behind the door, so that they will not see you when they open it."

"You do not want me to overpower them, I hope, Mr. Wood. They are very big, rough men."

"All I want you to do is grab their torches. They won't be expecting it. We've got used to the darkness. They haven't. We shall try to slip past and lock them in the cell. If we can't do that, I shall try to get one of their guns."

"There will be bloodshed and violence," predicted Mr. Gopal.

"Well, don't forget Professor Schumann," said Chip brusquely. "There's been bloodshed and violence already and they started it."

There was a moment's silence.

"You make me ashamed, Mr. Wood," said Mr. Gopal. "I have not been a great admirer of the British because they can be very violent people. But this time I think the British way is right. There must sometimes be bloodshed and violence, I fear. Ay, ay."

"Good for you, Mr. Gopal," said Chip, relieved. "How long before the guards bring the food?"

"Not yet. Two-three hours. Who can tell in the dark?"

"Right! Then let's work our way down to the entrance. We'll tell the others what we want them to do as we go."

This proved more difficult than it sounded. Chip found it hard to crawl through the holes which had been scooped out between the cells and several times he became stuck and had to be rescued. Also, to conceal the holes from the guards the prisoners had covered them with the twigs and straw they were allowed for bedding and many of them were sleeping, out of sheer boredom. They did not take very kindly to being awoken by Mr. Gopal suddenly burrowing up through their beds. To add to the other problems, most of the natives could speak only a few words of French and had difficulty in understanding when Mr. Gopal explained what was expected of them.

However, when they did understand, they were easily persuaded and, in fact, became quite enthusiastic at having something to do. They seemed gentle, childlike people, and Chip found difficulty in connecting them with the rioters in S. Jean. He guessed that Mr. Gopal had been right in suggesting that they became fiercer in a mob with a leader.

Even so, in spite of their easy-going nature, it was uphill work organising them in the dark, and by the time it was finished Chip was perspiring freely.

He arranged for the first six cells to be empty. He and Mr. Gopal were to be in the seventh. The prisoners from the empty cells were distributed among those farther from the shaft entrance. Chip crossed his fingers. He was counting heavily on the guards panicking when they discovered that six of the prisoners had apparently vanished.

"That's it, Mr. Gopal," he said finally. "Now all we have to do is wait. When the guards arrive I'll be flat out on the floor and you'll be behind the door where you can't be seen. Let's hope they'll be curious enough to unlock the door. They should be. After all, the one who brought me in will know that this is not my cell, and he'll want to know how I got in here, won't he?"

"Let us hope so," said Mr. Gopal, his teeth chattering slightly at the thought. "Mr. Wood, may I suggest a slight change of plan? I think it would be desirable if you take the torches and I pretend to be dead. This I could do more easily, I feel."

Chip thought rapidly. He guessed the guards would be more interested in him than in Mr. Gopal, but if Mr. Gopal lost his nerve and did not grab the guards' torches, the whole plan would come to nothing.

"No, we'll keep it as it is, Mr. Gopal," he decided finally. "Once the guard is in the cell, I'll try to help you. It'll be all right, you'll see."

With that, they settled down on the floor to wait. Chip could feel the air of expectancy in the other prisoners, who were giggling and chattering excitedly. Mr. Gopal clicked away to himself and cleared his throat nervously from time to time, but seemed unwilling to talk. The wait seemed endless in the dark, and the stale air was making Chip's head spin. He leaned back against the wall and closed his eyes. He knew he was scared, but he knew too that he was not going to let Mandrake down. He had done all he could and he forced himself not to worry about the danger ahead. To occupy himself he started thinking of the legend of Xarpata and his two wives. It was odd how it had stuck in his mind. He wondered whether there was any truth in it. Sometimes these old stories were based on fact, and he began to feel uneasy, trying to think of some hidden meaning.

He must have dozed off for he suddenly roused with Mr. Gopal shaking him.

"Wake up, Mr. Wood! They are here. Ay, ay. Why does he not awaken?" The beam of a torch was showing faintly through the grille and tins were being clattered at the entrance of the shaft. The other prisoners had fallen silent. The atmosphere quivered with tension.

"Quick, by the door, Mr. Gopal," he hissed. It could only be a few seconds before the guards discovered the empty cells.

He flung himself on the floor, face downwards, head towards the door and one leg drawn up, so that he would be ready to leap to Mr. Gopal's assistance when the moment came—if it came.

There was an unbearable delay. The guards stopped crashing about with the tin bowls. Chip tensed himself. Then the silence was shattered.

"*Sacré Tonnerre! Viens vite, Marchant!*"

Heavy feet thudded along the shaft as the guards rushed to check the other cells.

"*Ils se sont tous échappés, Marchant.*"

Chip shut his eyes and lay motionless. The footsteps

came to a halt. Even with his face to the ground he could
see the torch flashing through the grille and playing on him.
After more shouting, the second guard came up to look. This
was the critical moment. Everything now depended on
whether the door was opened right away, or whether the
guards decided to raise the alarm. Chip held his breath. He
heard Mr. Gopal click nervously, and willed him to be quiet.

Keys jangled. The lock squeaked rustily, and then the
door creaked open.

Chip forced himself to wait until the guard came right
into the cell. Then he leapt. His head well down, he butted
the guard full in the stomach and grabbed at the torch. The
man gasped like a punctured tyre and went over backwards,
slamming his companion against the wall. Chip tore the
torch free and sprang over him.

"Mr. Gopal!" he yelled. "Quick!"

He felt the Indian shoot past him like a startled rabbit
out into the shaft.

"I have it, Mr. Wood," twittered Mr. Gopal. "I have it,
sir."

What he had, Chip did not wait to discover. Instead he
slammed the cell door behind him and turned the key. Then
he doubled along the other cells, releasing the prisoners,
who by this time were screaming and shouting like a troop
of monkeys.

The first thing was to get them out of the guards' line
of fire. It would be a matter of only moments before they
recovered and started shooting. They were not likely to
discover the tunnels, as the entrances had been carefully
covered.

He pushed and shoved the prisoners towards the shaft
entrance. They were laughing and joking as though their
troubles were over, without any thought of what they should
do next.

Once they were out of immediate danger, Chip elbowed his way through, determined to get to the entrance first. The whole scheme would come to nothing if they just burst aimlessly out into the camp. There was still the security fence and the other guards with their dogs to be dealt with.

He put his back to the shaft door.

"Mr. Gopal," he yelled above the din. "Where are you?" He flashed the torch over the mass of bodies trying to push past him and saw Mr. Gopal at the back, jumping up and down to catch his attention. Mr. Gopal was very short, but not difficult to pick out in the confusion, because, unlike the other prisoners who were dressed in rags, he was wearing a crumpled white suit. His high-pitched voice could be heard above the general hubbub.

"Mr. Wood . . . here . . . not leave me . . . Mr. Wood . . ." He was waving something which looked to Chip suspiciously like a revolver. An instant later, as though to confirm the suspicion, there was a deafening explosion. In the confined space it sounded like a field-gun firing. Immediately there was a panic-stricken hush. For a moment Chip thought that the guards had finally come into action, but then he realised that it was Mr. Gopal who had fired the shot.

The little Indian seized the opportunity to squeeze through the press until he was beside Chip.

"Where did you get it?" demanded Chip.

"Mr. Wood, I tried to tell you. I took it from one of the guards as we were exiting from the cell. Please do not be angry. I did not mean to . . ."

"It doesn't matter," said Chip. "Just keep these lads back for half a tick. I want to see what's going on outside." He eased back the door and peered out. The interior of the camp was in complete darkness, except for the guardhouse, which was brilliantly lit. The perimeter fence was illuminated, too, by lights mounted on poles at regular intervals. Chip's heart was beating like a drum. The prison guards were bound to be missed before long and someone sent to see what was holding them up. He looked about anxiously for a way of escape.

The only route offering any hope at all was the exposed hill face. For the first hundred feet or so it had been cut away and formed a nearly vertical cliff. It was too dark to see whether there were footholds for the ascent. The only alternative was for all the prisoners to make a concerted dash for the guardroom. That would certainly rouse the camp and bring all the native workers out from their huts, but whether they would have the nerve to join in the attack and crush the armed guards by sheer numbers, was more than doubtful. If they had wanted, they could have tried it before.

Chip decided to reconnoitre the cliff-face. He waved to Mr. Gopal to keep the prisoners quiet, and, ignoring the Indian's horrified expression, crept out through the shaft door into the open air.

He moved cautiously along the foot of the cliff, his hand outstretched before him, feeling his way.

Then the entire hill seemed to fall on him. He lay, completely winded, too dazed even to wonder what had happened. Massive hands clamped round his throat.

"One squeak, one little squeak, Syndicate feller," rumbled a familiar voice in his ear, "and you're a gone goose."

A thrill of recognition ran through Chip.

"King," he croaked, "It's me."

The pressure on his throat relaxed.

"Is it you, young Chip? I came looking for you, boy. Thought you were in the lock-up down there."

"How did you get in, King," whispered Chip, incredulously.

"Down the cliff, boy. I got me a rope down the cliff. But don't let's stand here conversationalising. We've got to get out and back to Dr. Mandrake. He's mighty worried about you."

"Wait, King. I can't just go like that," said Chip, and rapidly explained about Mr. Gopal and the other prisoners.

"You mean forty-fifty stupid natives are just waiting inside that door?"

"That's it. What are we going to do? We can't just leave them, and they can't all climb your rope. The guards would spot them."

"Forty-fifty," rumbled King, and then forgetting the need for silence, suddenly let out a bellow of laughter. "That's a lot of men. With that number we could sure strike the oppressor, like Mr. Liberté would say. Stay here, young Chip and keep watch, while I say a few words to them natives."

He padded away eagerly to the door of the shaft. A few minutes later his deep voice could be heard thundering inside the shaft, alternating with the piping tones of Mr. Gopal, who was presumably translating the call to action into French. Chip waited uneasily. He would have preferred a quieter way out. He did not fancy their chances against the armed guard. The natives might be all right for rioting and fighting in the streets, but whether they could stand up to determined resistance was another matter. If they had that sort of spirit, he thought wryly, they would never have allowed themselves to be shut up and treated like cattle in the first place.

The light from the perimeter showed the darkened huts to be barred on the outside. He guessed the workers had been locked in for the night, already. The only movement was a guard passing under the lights, slowly patrolling the wired fence. The glowing tip of a cigarette showed that the man was taking things easily and expecting no trouble. He looked as though he was out for a quiet evening stroll with his dog.

It was the guardroom Chip watched nervously. At any moment someone must be sent to look for the two imprisoned guards. If Mr. Gopal, King, and the other prisoners were still in the shaft when that happened, they would be trapped, because one determined man could easily keep the entrance covered until reinforcements arrived.

Just as he had decided to hurry King up, the shaft door flew back. King strode out, towering above the prisoners who swarmed after him.

"When I give the word, fellers," ordered King, "Follow me." He waited impatiently until they were all clear of the shaft, then gave a defiant roar, which echoed from the cliff-face, and raced ahead straight towards the guardroom. His ebony face was split in a huge grin at the prospect of coming battle.

Chip had started after the advancing mass, when a dishevelled white-clad figure staggered from the shaft entrance. Mr. Gopal's small and bony frame shook with fright and rage. His thin grey hair stood out in spikes round his linen hat.

"Ay, ay," he wailed. "I tried to stop him, Mr. Wood. But he picked me up and threw me through the air. Who is he, that terrible man?"

"Never mind now. Come on, after them."

Already the prisoners, with King at their head, were half-way to the guardroom. Several had detached themselves from the main body and were streaking along the huts, unbarring the doors to free the workers.

"Shortly there will be much violence, Mr. Wood," panted Mr. Gopal.

Chip nodded fiercely. What he suddenly wanted above

F.M.   D

everything else was much violence, to fight the black uniforms face to face. He sprinted ahead and was at King's heels as the negro leapt the guardroom steps.

Without pausing to see whether anyone was with him, King charged across the veranda and, with one mighty blow, smashed open the door.

There must have been six or seven guards inside, gathered round Petit. He was questioning a prisoner, encouraging the terrified native with his knife, his wizened face wrinkled with pleasure at the pain he was inflicting. The guards were so intent on the entertainment, that they had no chance to recover before King was on them. He seized the table, flexed his gleaming muscles, and swung it around his head, batting them away like flies.

"Come on, black trousers," he bellowed. "Come on. Fight me!"

Three of them accepted his invitation, while a fourth, rolling clear, loosed a revolver from his belt.

Without hesitation, Chip dived on him and they threshed about together amid the stamping boots. The man proved too heavy, and pinning Chip, tried to club him with the revolver butt. He swung his arm up, hesitated for a second, and then collapsed sideways to the floor.

"Are you all right?" asked Mr. Gopal, a wild glint in his eye and his teeth bared in a nervous grin. He brandished the revolver he had taken in the mine shaft, looking round for fresh victims. But he was too late, for King was disposing of the last of them. He was holding the screaming Petit above his head.

"Go, small man, go!" bellowed King happily, and hurled Petit through the window.

The frame and glass splintered out into the darkness, leaving a gaping hole, through which came the chanting and shouts of the mob outside. King laughed, his face shining with sweat.

"Now for the black trousers at the fence," he chuckled, as though another treat was in store. "They won't know from nothing, young Chip, not from nothing."

Chip blocked his way.

"King," he shouted. "We've got to get to Dr. Mandrake. That's our first job, to get away from here."

King's smile broadened.

"Surely, surely . . ."

A fusillade of shots cut him short. For a moment there was complete silence, then screams of panic, above which Chip recognised the baying and snarling of the guard dogs.

King quivered, his smile gone. "Keep close, Chip, real close," he growled, and swung through the shattered window. Chip scrambled after him, followed by Mr. Gopal.

"Here, Mr. Wood, take these, please. I have made a collection from the guards."

The collection consisted of the guards' revolvers. In spite of the danger, Chip grinned.

"Thought you only believed in peaceful resistance, Mr. Gopal?"

"I do, Mr. Wood, I do. I am deeply ashamed. I have such a weak character. It is a disgrace."

King was already at the corner of the hut, taking stock of the situation. The gates of the compound were off their hinges and the way to freedom was open. But beyond, on the edge of the area illuminated by the perimeter lights, the guards had mustered with their dogs. Four crumpled figures lay under the Syndicate's mailed fist hanging over the gateway, a warning to anyone trying to rush the gap.

Chip guessed that the guards were not yet sure whether the natives had taken any arms from the guardroom, and therefore were not risking an advance. Once they decided that they could safely get through the gateway themselves, they would soon regain the mastery.

He grabbed two of the revolvers from Mr. Gopal, and passed one to King.

"We've got to go now, otherwise it will be too late," he urged.

"You're right, young Chip. We got to make a dash for that gate. When I get my hands on them black trousers, you don't worry. I'll deal with them."

"We can't do that," snapped Chip angrily. He realised that it was up to him to make a decision. King might be all right in a free-for-all, but when his blood was up he was just as likely to get them into trouble as out of it. "They'd just shoot us down. They can fire straighter than us if we're running. They've had more practice, anyhow. You go first. Mr. Gopal and me, we'll give you covering fire to keep their heads down. When you're through, you keep them busy and we'll join you." He glanced towards the natives, sheltering behind the huts, waiting to see what happened. "If they see us get through, they'll come too. Then the guards will have their work cut out. All right? Wait until we start firing before making a run for it."

King grunted approvingly, and dropping on hands and knees, crawled towards the lighted area.

"Mind you don't hit King," said Chip anxiously to Mr. Gopal, who was nerving himself to start shooting. He was holding his revolver as far away as he could and had an agonised expression on his bony face.

Chip waited till King was near the lights, then raised his revolver and fired. The kick nearly broke his wrist, but he gritted his teeth and pulled the trigger again and again.

The guards dived for cover, as he had hoped, but what he had not expected them to do was release the mastiffs at the same time. Directly King saw the guards go to the ground he launched himself at the gateway.

He met the dogs half-way, just under the lights. There were two of them, heavy, savage brutes. They sprang, snarling viciously, and knocked him from his feet. Chip dashed forward to get close enough to risk a shot. But before he had covered half the distance, King was up again, clutching the dogs by their throats. He heaved them into the air and, with a swing of his massive shoulders, flung them like toys away into the darkness.

Chip raced past him, firing in the direction of the guards. He heard a roar from the prisoners as they saw the way the fight was going, and he knew that they would follow.

Mr. Gopal, just behind, was blazing away wildly. One of his bullets whined overhead, too close for comfort. Chip shouted to him to stop, but the little Indian was too excited to notice and continued firing until his revolver was empty. The guards took to their heels when they saw the main body of prisoners breaking out. Even armed as they were, they were no match for several hundred natives, and they knew it.

King came up, wiping blood from his chest where one of the dogs had caught him.

"That was fine," he grinned. "Just fine, young Chip. Now let's get away from here."

He led the way at a rapid trot along the front of the escarpment, keeping well away from the dirt road. He struck out uphill, across the lower slopes. A few hundred yards on he stopped and waited for the others to catch up.

"Where are we going, King?" panted Chip.

After the excitement of the battle he suddenly felt empty and tired, more like lying down and sleeping than setting off on a route march.

"To Professor Schumann's house. We're going to meet

Mr. Liberté and your Dr. Mandrake there. They'll be waiting for us. Maybe ten-twenty miles. I don't know, not far."

Chip's heart sank. Ten-twenty miles. Not far!

Mr. Gopal toiled up to join them. Like Chip he seemed to be feeling the worse for wear.

"Please," he panted. "This is not possible. I wish to rest now. I think you must leave me behind, Mr. Wood, although I do not wish to be left alone. Indeed, not."

"Leave you behind, Mr. Gopal?" said Chip, secretly relieved that he had not been the one to call a halt. "Not on your life. Is there somewhere we can hide up for a breather, King?"

King thought for a moment.

"Too close to the camp here, fellers. Two-three miles farther on the trees begin. We could stop there for a while, I reckon."

Mr. Gopal sighed loudly.

"If you say so, Mr. King."

King chuckled. "You get too tired, you tell me. I'll carry you, Mr. Gopal. You too, Chip. Man, I feel good. I just need action to keep me healthy." Still chuckling, he led the way up the hill.

CHAPTER EIGHT

TERROR IN THE FOREST

CHIP WOKE with a start. He could not tell whether he had dreamed the explosion, or whether it had really happened.

A moment later the valley below glowed with a flickering light.

"What is it, Mr. Wood?" exclaimed Mr. Gopal, suddenly wide awake. "What has happened?"

Chip rubbed the sleep from his eyes and crawled out from the coppice where they had been resting. He went as far as the edge of the escarpment, and looked down.

Far below, a group of buildings were burning. The fire blazed up as a series of explosions ran through them. The skeleton of a crushing plant was silhouetted against the flames as the hills rang with the detonations.

"It must be King," he called. "I bet he went down there while we were asleep."

"This was foolish, Mr. Wood. Now we shall have the police after us, again. Ay, ay. They will guess which way we have gone."

Chip bit his lip impatiently. He knew that Mr. Gopal was right. They had been lucky to get so far and now King had queered their pitch while they had been sleeping.

"I hope he gets away. Otherwise we'll be stuck here. How can we find our way to Professor Schumann's house if he doesn't come?"

"You forget, Mr. Wood, that I know the way," said Mr. Gopal reproachfully, adding doubtfully, "At least, I think so. It is true I have never been across the hills at night. Yis, we shall become lost, you are right."

Chip waved him to be quiet. There was movement on the hillside just below them.

"Fellers," came a hoarse whisper through the darkness. "Is that you, fellers?"

A few seconds later King was beside them. He laid a bulging sack on the ground and squatted down, chuckling happily.

"You ready to get moving?" he asked breathlessly. "Better not hang around here. Black trousers will be along in next to no time." He straightened up again, swung the sack over his shoulder, and had one last look down at the fire.

"What did you do it for, King?" demanded Chip angrily. "You knew it would put them on to us again."

King started to laugh, then hung his head, ashamed. "Sorry, young Chip," he muttered. "Guess I got kinda bored with you asleep like that."

To forestall any further rebuke he strode on ahead, leaving Chip and Mr. Gopal to follow. There was nothing to be done about King. Chip remembered how Richard Liberté had chided him for the riot in S. Jean, and Mandrake's comment, "A noble savage." Blowing up the Syndicate's property because he was bored. Chip grinned to himself. He felt fresh and suddenly cheerful. Maybe King had the right idea after all.

The going was good, over firm springy turf, as they turned eastwards, skirting the woods. The air was cool and clear and the sky was already lightening ahead of them. They were able to set a good pace and keep it up for several miles.

King slackened his stride and looked back. "You O.K. fellers?" he beamed. "Not far now. Another ten-fifteen miles, I reckon."

Fortunately, he proved to have only the vaguest idea of distance. The journey took just over three hours, during which, Chip estimated, they covered not more than six miles. After an hour or so their route crossed rocky, broken terrain, which slowed them down. When dawn came, he was able to take stock of their surroundings. The country was lush and wild, riven with steep defiles and surmounted by rocky outcrops. The lower slopes were thickly wooded and colourful with tropical vegetation, while the air was alive with birds of brilliant plumage. In fact, it was difficult to believe that a constant threat hung over them. Chip had to remind himself of the sinister figure on the yacht who, even now, must be taking steps to recapture them. But he was not allowed to forget their danger for long.

"Careful fellers," growled King. "Black trousers."

He pointed down into the ravine they were descending. Chip glimpsed two armed police guarding the crossing of the narrow torrent racing through the rocks. A wooden hut with the mailed fist emblem painted on the side, by the ford, suggested that it was a regular post. Two other black-uniformed figures with a dog were just moving off towards the mines. It cost half an hour to detour and find an unguarded crossing farther south, away from the direction the patrol had taken.

Twice more there were signs of the Syndicate police before Mr. Gopal started clicking excitedly.

"There! There is the house of Professor Schumann, Mr. Wood."

He pointed across the brow of a low hill to where a grey, heavy building could be seen, lying below a rocky crag.

King turned and waved urgently for them to get down. "Maybe it's young Richard and your Dr. Mandrake, I don't see too clear; but there's some people at the house. You stay here while I make sure we don't walk into nothing. Don't want to take no chances."

He plunged off the track and disappeared into the undergrowth.

"It looks more like a fort than a house," Chip said, staring at the grim buildings.

"Yis, this is what it was, Mr. Wood. All along the Copper Belt the settlers built forts to protect the mines and the northern part of the island from the Gardiens. Very fierce people."

"Weren't you and Professor Schumann afraid they would attack you, living here like this?"

Mr. Gopal's face, grey with fatigue, lit up enthusiastically.

"No, no, Mr. Wood. I told you, it is many, many years since the Gardiens left the forest. In any case, Professor Schumann was their friend. They trusted him. Very respected man. He spent much time in the forests with them. You cannot see from here, Mr. Wood, but beyond these hills are their forests, all the way to the mountains in the south of the island."

Chip looked up warily. Someone was coming through the undergrowth in a great hurry, from the direction King had taken. The bushes parted and there stood Mandrake, looking dishevelled but very determined.

"Chip, Chip," he exclaimed. "Upon my soul, I am vastly relieved to see you." When he gripped Chip's shoulders his hands were trembling. He peered at Chip as though examining a rare archæological specimen for damage.

"All right, boy? Not hurt?"

Chip grinned and shook his head. He had had no idea how glad he would be to see the lean figure of the doctor again. But there was one question that needed an immediate answer.

"You didn't give in to Malik, did you, Dr. Mandrake?

You didn't agree to help him on my account, did you?"

Mandrake shook his head.

"Greatly tempted. Never have forgiven myself had you been harmed. But Richard Liberté and that splendid black man . . ."

"King," prompted Chip.

"A most suitable name . . . persuaded me to let them try to free you, before I agreed to the detestable Malik's terms. A most wise decision." He peered over Chip's shoulder at Mr. Gopal. "Who is this? I've seen him before." Chip guessed that the sudden fierceness of his tone was put on to balance his recent show of feeling. Chip introduced Mr. Gopal, who clicked politely and referred to Mandrake's earlier visit to Professor Schumann.

"Excellent memory. Most flattered. That is many years ago. Remember you perfectly though. Most grateful for your help. Let us all go to the house of poor Julius. Richard Liberté is there. You must be exceedingly hungry, and we are pressed for time."

Chip suddenly realised that he *was* exceedingly hungry. He hurried eagerly down the track, explaining to Mandrake what had happened, as they went.

They found King sitting on the terrace eating provisions from a box of supplies. He grinned hugely and waved for them to join him.

"Dig in, fellers," he mumbled. "Or there won't be nothing left."

Chip accepted the invitation, seizing a wing of game and a hunk of black bread. In spite of the unfamiliar, seasoned flavour of the meat and the bitterness of the bread, he thought he had never tasted more delicious food. Mr. Gopal shook his head disapprovingly and, selecting a handful of nuts and dried fruit for himself, disappeared into the house.

When the sharper pangs of hunger had been satisfied, Chip looked up at Mandrake, who had been watching him with an unusually amiable expression, nodding approvingly from time to time.

"What's going to happen now, Dr. Mandrake? What are we going to do?"

"Do? Going into the forest to seek out the Gardiens. Now convinced that whatever Julius Schumann discovered, it was in the southern part of the island. Thought about it carefully and that is the only possibility. Come, I will take you up to the roof for a brief glimpse of where we are going."

Mandrake led the way through a sagging french window that had lost its glass, into a long and lofty room furnished as a study. Everything was in wild disorder. Broken chairs and tables, hundreds of books torn to pieces, littered the floor. Pictures in shattered frames, lay with their canvases slashed to ribbons. The only articles spared were native ceremonial masks and cloaks in a thick, grey material, which hung around the walls.

A small, desolate figure stood in one corner.

"Look, Mr. Wood. Look what they have done to the distinguished Professor's home."

Tears ran down Mr. Gopal's thin features.

"Ay, ay," he wailed. "They are most evil men."

Chip looked inquiringly at Mandrake.

"Syndicate police," explained Mandrake in an undertone. "Searched the place after killing Julius."

He patted Mr. Gopal's back sympathetically, before leading off along a narrow gallery to an open timber staircase.

As they came out on the flat roof into the brilliant sunlight Chip caught his breath, for the whole southern part of the island, the land of the Gardiens, lay before him.

The roof had been constructed as a lookout platform for

the fort. It commanded a wide expanse of forest, which ran down from the Copper Belt to stretch, like an undulating sea of green, until it was lost in shimmering haze. At first, Chip thought the southern horizon was obscured by heavy cloud, but Mandrake pointing to the dark mass said:

"Convinced the key to all this is up there, Chip, somewhere in the mountains of the Gardiens."

As he spoke, the mists parted momentarily and Chip saw that what he had taken for clouds were, in fact, distant mountains, far higher and more imposing than any hills in the north of the island. He had a fleeting glimpse of a glittering snow-capped peak, apparently floating in the upper air. He gazed fascinated by the strange, remote spectacle.

"Is that the Flashing Mountain?" he asked, breathlessly.

"No, Mr. Wood. It is somewhere in that range, but it cannot be seen from here. It is really only a pillar of rock, not a mountain at all. Professor Schumann told me this." Unnoticed, Mr. Gopal had followed them to the roof. He looked sadly out across the forests. "He spoke often of the mountains and the Gardiens before he died. He spent much time with them there."

"Ever go with him?" asked Mandrake.

Mr. Gopal shook his head.

"He would not let me do so, sir. I looked after the house. There was much work."

"Ever tell you that he had seen the Flashing Mountain?"

Mr. Gopal shook his head again.

"He told me a long time ago that the Gardiens had agreed to allow him to go there. I thought he was to do this the last time he went into the forests. But when he returned, he said nothing to me. He was strange and worried. And now he is dead. Ay, ay."

"This was two or three months ago?" asked Mandrake.

He reminded Chip of a dog suddenly taking a scent. "He was worried after returning from a journey to the Gardiens which may have taken him to the Flashing Mountain?"

"Yis," said Mr. Gopal. "This is so."

"About the time he wrote and asked me to come," nodded Mandrake, half to himself. "It fits. It fits. Richard Liberté could not tell me, since he did not see Julius after this last journey."

This reminded Chip that he had as yet seen no trace of Richard.

"Where is he, Dr. Mandrake? I thought he was here?"

"So he is. Down at the edge of the forest. He brought some natives from S. Jean as porters for us. They've brought Julius Schumann's equipment. Might be useful. Any case, determined not to let Malik get his hands on it. Sure it would give him a clue as to what Julius was after. Dare not risk leaving it behind."

"And the Syndicate let them pass?"

Mandrake gave a short bark of laughter.

"I'll say this for young Liberté, he has a gift for organisation. The Syndicate knew nothing about it until long after we had left. Mustn't hang around here too long, either. Bound to look here for us. Obvious place."

"Ay, ay. How true this is," wailed Mr. Gopal suddenly. "Be good enough to look there, gentlemen."

He pointed upward to a rock turret a hundred feet above and behind them. Outlined against the brassy sky was the heavy, unmistakable shape of Jason Kreamer, and by his side the dwarf-like figure of Petit. Mandrake did not hesitate.

"Out!" he snapped. "We must get away from here and join Richard Liberté in the forest at once."

Chip grabbed Mr. Gopal's arm and dragged him to the stairway. They raced after Mandrake, down the stairs, out across the terrace. Mr. Gopal tore his arm from Chip's grasp.

"Do not wait, Mr. Wood. I have forgotten something. Most important. I will follow, one minute," he panted, and darted back into the house.

He was as good as his word, for scarcely a minute later he reappeared carrying a bundle of the native costumes, which had lately been on the study walls.

Mandrake came running back across the terrace, having discovered that they were not following him.

"At once, Charles Wood," he shouted angrily. "Do as I say, sir. We are in great danger here."

Chip seized the bundle from Mr. Gopal, pushing him on ahead, towards the cover of the trees.

At the bottom of the slope, in a clearing, they found Richard Liberté and his party. It consisted of eleven or twelve natives in tattered European clothes, who had obviously been pressed into service. They looked pretty discontented and reluctant about the expedition. King was sorting out the loads they were to carry and his heavy-handed good humour was doing little to dispel their sullenness.

"It was to be expected," said Liberté, when told of the appearance of Kreamer and Petit. "As you say, Dr. Mandrake, this was an obvious place for them to search. Well, your party is ready. I would advise that you leave at once, then you will be able to cover ten or twelve miles before dark."

"Aren't you coming with us?" demanded Chip. He felt already that he had known Liberté for a long time. Liberté shook his head. He looked solemn and intense, as though he had the worries of the world on his shoulders.

"It would not be wise. I must return to S. Jean. Otherwise the people will get out of hand and give the Syndicate excuse for even more repressive measures. Conditions are very delicate. When we strike, it must be with maximum effect. I shall send King with you to look after the porters— and to keep him out of the way." He handed Mandrake a sporting rifle he had been carrying, and held out his hand. "*Au revoir et bonne chance!*"

The porters shouldered their loads, which had been strung on poles so that each box was carried by two men, and slowly wound their way down into the forest.

The last they saw of Liberté was as he stood at the edge of the clearing, gravely watching their departure. Then, with a brief wave he was gone.

Chip, King, and Mr. Gopal settled down to a steady pace at the head of the column, while Mandrake stalked up and down its length, barking irritably at the porters. They paid little or no attention to him, but plodded onward with downcast eyes and resentful expressions.

"It would be ungrateful to criticise, but these porters Richard Liberté has chosen do not seem very suitable," Mandrake said testily.

"Chosen ain't the right word, Dr. Mandrake," said King. "They wouldn't come into these forests if they could help it. They're real scared of the Gardiens. They came because the police were after them in S. Jean. Mr. Liberté offered to help them get away if they would help you. Simple as that."

"Don't trust them," muttered Mandrake. "Must keep a close eye on them, otherwise they'll be off."

Still grumbling to himself, he dropped back, taking up station at the rear of the column, so that he could better keep an eye on his reluctant helpers.

Chip stared about curiously. He had not really known what to expect in the forest and had imagined a tangled mass of bush, teeming with reptiles and wild animals.

Instead, he found a dim maze with little light penetrating through the leaves of the great trees that towered sixty or seventy feet above their heads. There was little under-growth between the trunks, only a thick, soft carpet laid down by centuries of decaying vegetation. As for wild life, the only sign was the chattering and whooping of the birds alarmed at the approach of the party. Their cries echoed beneath the canopy of leaves, as though it were the vaulted roof of a great building. King laughed when Chip told him what he had been expecting.

"Don't go getting wrong ideas, young Chip," he chuckled. "We're still quite high up here. Farther in, the forest gets real mean. Down near the river there are swamps and such-like, snakes and other creatures, so I've heard tell."

"This is true," said Mr. Gopal. "Professor Schumann said so. That is why, really, I did not accompany him on his journeys."

"Probably one of the reasons why they aren't happy about coming along on ours," grinned Chip, jerking his thumb at the porters.

"Yis," agreed Mr. Gopal. "I understand how they feel. May I now make a suggestion? Professor Schumann said that he always stopped after the first hour or so to check the loads. Otherwise his porters complained they came undone, and used this as an excuse to steal things. He must have done this about here." He pointed to some lengths of cord and a broken slat from a packing case, lying beside the track.

"I thought Professor Schumann went on these journeys alone. Did he have porters then?"

"Only as far as the river," replied Mr. Gopal. "From there he went on alone, always alone. His porters waited at the river for his return."

They dropped back to join Mandrake, who agreed to call a halt. He was in a better humour after the uneventful progress of the first hour. He personally checked that the equipment boxes were securely lashed, leaving King to make sure of the rest. The porters either lay down to rest, or wandered off among the trees looking for wild fruit and anything Professor Schumann's party might have left.

"What is that you've brought with you, Mr. Gopal?" asked Mandrake cheerfully, nodding at the bundle the little Indian had been at such pains to collect from the house.

Mr. Gopal smiled nervously and unrolled it on the ground, revealing two of the grey masks and ceremonial dresses, which had been hanging in the study.

"Professor Schumann said that he would never go to the Gardiens without these, Dr. Mandrake. I thought you should take them too."

Mandrake picked them up curiously.

"Remarkable! Appear to be some sort of paste worked into a woven base. Most unusual. Most thoughtful of you."

Chip examined the material. It was, as Mandrake had said, a grey rubbery material about two inches thick, stretched on canvas-like cloth. No attempt had been made at decoration and the whole effect was crude and even grotesque. It was designed to envelope completely the wearer, with a mask like a deep sea diver's helmet. Slits for the eyes were at the bottom of great blister-like protuberances, so that the wearer could see only a short distance in front of his feet.

"It looks more like an apron," he said at length. "Like they use in factories to protect people, than a get-up for ceremonies. You know, the sort of things welders use."

Mandrake glanced at him keenly, then back at the mask in his hand.

"A protective apron," he mused. "Brilliant observation,

Chip. That is . . ." He broke off and started to his feet as the silence of the forest was broken by a scream, an unspeakable, long, throbbing sound, so full of terror that Chip was rooted to the spot until long after it had died away. He felt Mr. Gopal's hand creep into his.

"What was it, Mr. Wood? This is not a good place."

After a moment's frozen silence, during which even the birds were still, the porters started chattering excitedly. They collected close together, as though for protection, and stared at Mandrake for reassurance and instructions.

"Count them, King," he rapped. "See if anyone is missing."

They waited anxiously while King numbered off the porters.

"One of them's gone, Dr. Mandrake, sir," he reported, grimly.

"Very well. We must find him. Not well equipped for this sort of thing, but we must try," said Mandrake, picking up his rifle.

"We'll take some of this, fellers," murmured King, rummaging in his sack and drawing out a handful of short red sticks.

"What's that?" snapped Mandrake.

"Dynamite, Dr. Mandrake, sir. I took it from the mines. Might come in useful."

"Useful! Well, never mind now. Don't blow us all up, that's all." Mandrake led the way through the trees, with King at his shoulder and Chip and Mr. Gopal just behind. One or two of the hardier porters trailed along at a safe distance. They advanced cautiously in the direction from which the cry had come. It was difficult to fix an accurate bearing and they spread out slightly. The absence of undergrowth and the wide spacing of the trees made any surprise attack unlikely. In fact, a short inspection showed that there was no one, besides themselves, in the area. Mr. Gopal clung to Chip's hand as though expecting a nameless horror to leap upon him at any instant.

"There! I seen him. Over there," shouted King suddenly, and rushing on ahead, plunged into a shallow gully.

By the time the others had caught up with him he was bending over the missing porter, who was lying motionless on his face at the bottom of the depression.

"He's a dead man," growled King. "Better come down and see, Dr. Mandrake." Carefully he started to turn the porter over, then, with a startled grunt, he dropped the body and leapt back, for the dead man's face had turned into a hideous mask, grey and rubbery like the costumes of the Gardiens.

CHAPTER NINE

LAND OF THE GARDIENS

THE OTHER porters, on seeing the fate of their companion, turned and fled like one man, back along the track to the copper hills. Evidently they preferred the familiar miseries of the Syndicate to the unknown terror stalking the forest.

"Let's face it," said Mandrake, as the last of them disappeared. "If we turn back now we shall have no second chance. Never find porters to come with us again, even if we do not immediately fall into the hands of the Syndicate ourselves. We are on the track of Julius Schumann's secret, I am convinced. Resolved to go on to find the Gardiens, alone, if necessary. But there is great danger, so you must each choose for yourselves. I will not attempt to persuade you. If you go back, Richard Liberté will hide you until you can escape from the island. Chip, what do you say?"

"I'll come with you, Dr. Mandrake," replied Chip, more confidently than he felt.

"King?"

The huge negro swallowed nervously, his usual cheerful features grave and troubled.

"I don't fancy it, Dr. Mandrake, sir," he mumbled. "I ain't afraid of nothing I can see, but I don't fancy this, and that's the truth. Don't you worry, though, I won't let you and young Chip go on by yourselves. I'm coming."

Mandrake nodded again, gratefully.

"Mr. Gopal?"

The little Indian rocked to and fro moaning unhappily.

"Yis, yis, I come with you," he said, through chattering

teeth. "Professor Schumann would have wished it. I do not wish it, for I am afraid, but I will come. But I fear that I am a great coward."

"Very well," said Mandrake, obviously relieved. "Grateful to you all. First thing to do is find out what happened to this unfortunate fellow, if we can."

He bent over the body and examined the head and shoulders carefully. "Looks as though he has been exposed to some extraordinary force, some radiation that burned his face to ashes."

"Guess you're right at that, Dr. Mandrake," exclaimed King uneasily. "See up there."

He pointed to the branches overhanging the hollow. A patch of grey, withered foliage stood out clearly. "Whatever it was, burnt up them trees, too."

"Incredible!" exclaimed Mandrake. "He must have found something, bent over it and opened it, exposing himself and the trees above."

"Dr. Mandrake, Dr. Mandrake," called Mr. Gopal. "Come and see, quickly." He was on his hands and knees in a clump of ferns.

"Touch nothing," shouted Mandrake. "Nothing at all. What is it, Mr. Gopal?"

"This belonged to Professor Schumann. He took it on his last journey." He was pointing at a leaden casket, lying half-concealed, with broken and corroded laboratory instruments around it, in the ferns. The hinged lid was open, revealing an empty interior. Just beyond, was a hole in the ground, ringed with the distinctive grey substance.

"Don't go near the hole," ordered Mandrake. Using a stick, he closed the lid and picked up the casket by the carrying strap. "We'll take this with us. If Julius Schumann needed it, so may we. There's one comfort, we're in no immediate danger if this wretched man's death was an accident. Thought for a moment he'd been attacked. What the container was doing there, and why it was abandoned, is still an open question."

"This I think I know, Dr. Mandrake," said Mr. Gopal apologetically. "It was stolen when the evil men searched the house. Many things were stolen by them."

"Probably some of those Syndicate ruffians decided to keep part of the loot for themselves, instead of turning it all over to their masters. Brought it into the forest to examine, and threw away what was of no value to them. It was their fortune that they abandoned the casket without opening it."

"Bad luck for that feller," muttered King, looking uncomfortably at the dead porter.

"Indeed," said Mandrake. "But he is beyond our help. Now we must think of ourselves. First, we must select some supplies. Then we must be on our way. We shall not be able to carry much, but at least we shall travel more quickly."

They returned silently to the abandoned loads. Mandrake, who seemed more grimly determined than ever, estimated they would need enough supplies for at least six days. They sorted out the more compact boxes of food and took also a small portable cooker, which used tablets of solid fuel.

"We must leave the electronic equipment here. We will conceal it as best we can," decided Mandrake. "No great loss. I have only the vaguest idea of its function. Take your costumes and masks, Mr. Gopal. I have a feeling they are of importance. Sure of it."

Within half an hour they were on their way again. Although the party was now so small, at least they knew and trusted one another. The porters had been a doubtful element from the beginning and Chip had the feeling that they would be no loss. He edged up beside Mandrake, who was striding out in front.

"Where exactly are we heading for, Dr. Mandrake? Where do you expect to find the Gardiens?"

"First to their city in the forest, where I excavated when I was here before. Then perhaps to the mountains. We shall see."

"But I thought it was in ruins. Do they still live there?"

Mandrake frowned impatiently.

"As you say, it is in ruins. The Gardiens are now centred on their so-called sacred city in the mountains. But they left a small community behind at the old city. Their numbers are reducing all the time. One of the tragedies of civilisation, Chip. Happened many times with other tribes who were too proud, or too sensible, to take up with our ways."

"How long will it take to get there?"

"Last time, two days, but that was with equipment and porters. This time a day and a half—to-morrow evening, perhaps."

"Do you think they'll remember you? Suppose they just attack us. Everyone says they're dangerous."

Mandrake's beard jutted aggressively.

"I have excavated all over the world, Charles Wood. I have never stood impertinence from natives, fierce or otherwise. I do not intend to start now." His expression became so forbidding, that Chip dropped back to join King and Mr. Gopal once more. Mandrake's tone had suggested that he was not in the mood to stand impertinence from Chip either.

The next few hours proved such hard going that there was no opportunity for idle conversation. Chip did not feel much like it, anyhow. He kept thinking of what had happened to the dead porter and wondering uneasily what lay ahead. He knew Malik would have heard that the party had been spotted at Julius Schumann's house and must be laying plans for pursuit.

As King had predicted the nature of the forest changed, the farther they penetrated. For several miles the land dropped steadily, while the vegetation became thicker and wilder. Before long, they were no longer following a regular track, but pressing on in a generally south-westward direction.

"Want to reach the river before nightfall," explained Mandrake, during a brief halt. "Shall make camp there and to-morrow follow it upstream. That will take us to our destination. Must put as much distance as we can between ourselves and Kreamer, if he's following. Think it's doubtful myself. He'd need time to provision a party. But Malik will guess where we're making for. Sure of it. He'll think up something."

Chip glanced at their companions as they reshouldered their loads. He might have known that it would be Mr. Gopal who would be first on his feet and who would look freshest of them all.

"Dr. Mandrake," said Mr. Gopal. "I feel I am a great nuisance to you all. I am slowing you down. Please forgive me. You are most kind to allow me to accompany you."

Chip brushed the hair out of his eyes, swung his load up and grinned to himself. Good old Mr. Gopal, he never missed a chance.

The heat and humidity steadily increased. The sturdy forest trees of the highlands gave way to masses of shrubs, which, although bearing vivid colours, created a poisonous atmosphere with the heavy perfumes they exuded. The sickly air was filled with the whine of vicious insects circling tormentingly around eyes and mouths.

For the hundredth time, Chip wiped the perspiration from his face. If Mandrake was intending to make camp in this country, he thought wearily, they were in for a sleepless night. The only thing to be said for it, was the irritations and discomforts made it impossible to worry about Kreamer behind, or the Gardiens in front. The present was more than enough to be going on with.

At length, Mandrake halted, and waited for the others to come up with him.

"There," he said shortly. "There's the river."

They stared silently at a fifty-yard expanse of brown water, flowing sluggishly beneath overhanging branches. The surface was covered with all the debris of the forest, dead branches, matted leaves, and hummocks of grass. In fact, thought Chip, it looked more like a drain than a river.

"It is most beautiful," said Mr. Gopal. "In my country there are many rivers like this on the plains."

"Come," said Mandrake. "We must quickly make camp. It will soon be dark and then it will be too late."

They found a level promontory jutting into the river. It was rocky, free from vegetation and slightly higher than the adjoining land.

"Not ideal," announced Mandrake. "But it will serve."

They settled themselves as best they could and prepared food.

But before they could finish eating, the brief twilight gave way to night, the darkness coming down like a curtain. Chip was too tired to care much about eating, anyhow, and wearily sank back on the stony ground, using his pack of provisions as a pillow.

He fell asleep almost immediately but, after an hour or so, the hardness of the ground and the strange animal calls echoing through the forest roused him. He could tell by the restless movements of his companions, that they too, were having a disturbed night. Only Mr. Gopal seemed untroubled. A gentle, flute-like snoring showed that he was enjoying the sleep of the just.

"It's as bad as Clapham Junction," Chip muttered irritably to himself after a particularly hideous outcry in a clump of thorn nearby. Mandrake rolled over towards him.

"Stop biting your fingers, boy. Bad habit, must cure yourself. Can't sleep? Neither can I. But look up there, behind you. Never seen a finer sight. Twenty thousand feet if an inch."

Chip sat up. Above the tangle of trees, riding high over the clammy mists of the river, glittering in moonlight that did not penetrate the forest, was a slender snow-capped pinnacle, majestic and remote, like the entrance to another world.

"It's smashing, Dr. Mandrake," he whispered, present discomforts forgotten. "Just smashing."

"That's where we shall be going," replied Mandrake soberly. "I have been thinking hard while you have slept and I am convinced that Julius Schumann discovered that source of power, which destroyed the wretched porter to-day, somewhere in those mountains."

Chip sat up straighter. Suddenly his mind seemed as clear as crystal.

"Do you remember, in the book you gave me, Dr. Mandrake," he demanded excitedly. "When the god Xarpata hid in those mountains, he said he would *look* at anyone who disturbed him, and that they would die. That's like what happened to the porter, isn't it?"

"Ah, you remember that, Chip. There is usually some hidden meaning in these old legends. Yes, it fits. Now it remains for us to persuade the Gardiens to have as much confidence in us as they did in Julius Schumann."

Chip shifted his pack so that he could keep his eyes on

the distant mountain. Although he was now too excited for more sleep, or so he thought, it was not long before his eyes closed again and he dozed off to the accompaniment of Mandrake's voice, speaking, it seemed, half to himself.

Towards dawn Chip stirred uneasily. He was dreaming of being chased by the gang on the night he had boarded the *Salamander*. He was stumbling across the marshes again, with the burning hut behind him and the railway embankment in front. But, this time, it was different, because a train was coming. Somehow, he could not get across the line, no matter how hard he tried. He could hear the train pounding nearer and nearer. It was so close, the ground beneath him shuddered and trembled. In a panic, he awoke.

"Don't move," called Mandrake firmly. "It's a mild earth tremor. Nothing serious. The President said there had been several recently."

Twice more there was a drumming deep in the earth that made the birds scream with alarm and the foliage rustle as in a high wind. Then, as suddenly as it started, the disturbance was over.

Mandrake made little of it, but in the early morning light, his face was pale and drawn.

"As we're up early, we'll break camp and be on our way before the heat of the day," he said with determined cheerfulness.

Mr. Gopal prepared food, while the others washed at the river's edge.

"A terrible night, Mr. Wood," he said handing Chip a mug of steaming coffee. "I did not once close my eyes. Ay, ay."

Chip, remembering the gentle snores, smiled to himself, but said nothing.

They pushed on rapidly along the river bank for several

miles, until they encountered dense growths of cane blocking their path. No other way seemed open so they had to cut a path through it. Without King they would hardly have succeeded. He was happy at finding, for the first time since the journey had started, a problem that could be solved by sheer physical strength. Like a powerful machine he went through the cane, tirelessly slicing with powerful, rhythmic strokes of his massive shoulders. As they broke through the barrier, he grinned: "Gives me an appetite, fellers. I needed the exercise."

He seemed disappointed that there were no further obstacles for him to overcome.

They arrived without further incident at the ruins of the Gardiens' city, as Mandrake had predicted, by late afternoon. It was rather a disappointment to Chip, who had been expecting something more imposing. Only a few mounds of overturned masonry and a fortified earthwork remained, standing on a bluff overlooking the river. The wall of the vegetation on the landward side was pressing in, engulfing the ruins with thick, fleshy tentacles.

"More like a village than a city," said Chip.

Mandrake smiled sourly at this display of ignorance.

"Two thousand people once lived here. Their houses were of mud and cane. Completely disappeared now. This is the inner city, dwelling of the King, temple, granary, all within a central enclosure. Quite remarkable."

"Don't seem to be no one living here now, Dr. Mandrake, sir," said King. "Thought you said there was, sir."

"Six or seven huts on the far side, near the river, when I was here. Keep together. Show no signs of fear if we are approached. Make no sudden movements. I will deal with them."

These precautions were unnecessary as there was no sign of life, other than a lizard racing for cover at their approach.

The huts were still where Mandrake remembered them, but they too were in ruins. The mud walls had been washed away, exposing the cane framework, and the plaited roofs were stripped of covering.

King shook his head:

"Kind of ghostly here. I don't fancy it."

Chip peered in through the entrance of the best preserved hut, and then jumped back.

"Dr. Mandrake," he shouted. "There *is* someone here." He looked with awe at the massive figure that slowly crept from the opening and straightened up before him.

The Gardien must have been over seven feet tall, over-topping even King by several inches. His light brown skin was wrinkled and pock-marked. In spite of his great stature he was wasted and thin. He stood there, naked except for a loincloth, facing them like an animal at bay, his head turning slowly from side to side. Mandrake stepped up and spoke to him, first in French and then, haltingly, in a language unknown to Chip. But the Gardien not merely did not understand, he did not appear to hear. He kept turning his head vacantly from side to side and grunted gutturally.

"Dr. Mandrake," exclaimed Mr. Gopal. "This man will not hear you, for he is deaf. He is blind, also."

"Well, he must have heard us coming," frowned Man-drake.

"This is not so. He must have felt our footsteps on the ground. Those who are deaf and blind are very sensitive. I know this, for there are many such in my country."

The Gardien suddenly stretched out his arms, brushed against Chip, and seized him. Chip froze with terror. There was something eerie about the gnarled sightless face thrust into his. Mandrake put out a restraining hand as King started forward.

"Wait! Keep quite still, Chip."

The Gardien ran his fingers lightly over Chip's head and shoulders. When he felt the shirt he stopped, his face troubled and puzzled. Then he dropped his hands, threw back his head, and gave a great baying cry, that echoed across the river. The melancholy sound seemed to hang in the air. Then, as it died away, he turned and shuffled back through the entrance of his hut, as though his task were completed.

"Well," said Mandrake, breaking the silence that had fallen after the old man had disappeared. "So much for that." For once he seemed completely put out, and it was several moments before he could decide what to do next.

"We must go on directly," he continued at length. "No help for us here. No point in wasting our time."

As they turned away, Mr. Gopal took some packets of dried fruit from his bundle and put it by the entrance of the hut.

"I have little appetite," he explained apologetically. "It must be very difficult to be blind and alone."

Mandrake was very preoccupied as he led the way back to the river.

"What do you think, Dr. Mandrake," queried Chip anxiously. "When he shouted like that, was it a signal?"

"Maybe," replied Mandrake absently. "Perhaps."

"It's jolly funny that they should leave a blind man alone like that," persisted Chip.

"On the contrary, it's becoming all painfully clear," replied Mandrake. "But let us press on while the light still holds." He seemed depressed and worried by what had happened, so Chip let him go on alone.

By the time they made camp for the night they were already on rising ground above the swampy river basin, the first indication of the mountains ahead. Even this slight elevation gave them some relief from the suffocating humidity and mosquitoes, though not enough for comfort. There had been two further earth tremors during the afternoon but, apart from increasing the tension, the shocks did no damage and were quickly over.

As the party sat round the cooker eating their evening meal, Mandrake explained briefly that he intended pressing on to the Gardiens' city in the mountains, but he did not talk about the Flashing Mountain or, in fact, go into any details about what he hoped to do.

King and Mr. Gopal took the news quietly. Chip guessed they realised they had gone too far to turn back, even if they wanted to.

"Mountains are a pretty big place to look, Dr. Mandrake," observed King rather glumly. "'Less you know where you're going."

"We know the Gardiens' city is on a big lake. Follow the river towards its source, King. Obviously rises in the mountains. May very well start in their lake, which, almost certainly, is fed by snows farther up."

Mandrake made it sound simple, but Chip had a good idea he was much less confident than his brisk tone suggested. They stared silently up at the white-clad peak that seemed now to tower right above them. Beautiful it might be, menacing it certainly was. It looked like a sentinel, set to guard the Flashing Mountain from any rash intruder.

When at last Chip fell asleep he was too exhausted to feel the hardness of the ground, and slept like a log until morning. He was roused by Mr. Gopal.

"It is time to go, Mr. Wood. I have prepared food. It is not at all good, but it is hot, I think."

They continued their march, pushing on through dense woodland, with the ground rising sharply all the while.

Late in the morning Mandrake suddenly signalled for

silence. "Listen," he rapped. They stopped and strained their ears, but apart from the chatter of the birds and the wind sighing through the trees high above, Chip could hear nothing.

"What is it, Mr. Wood?" whispered Mr. Gopal. "Do you hear something?"

Mandrake waved impatiently for him to be still.

"There," he said after a moment. "There it is again."

"Sounds like an aeroplane, Dr. Mandrake," muttered King. "Kind of funny aeroplane, but that's what it must be."

Chip caught it too, an engine note with a heavy beat, which somehow was familiar.

"It's a helicopter," he said suddenly. "That's what they sound like. I've heard them flying up and down the Thames to South Bank. There was one on the *Midas*. Perhaps it's Kreamer looking for us."

The forests had almost driven the Syndicate from his mind. The sound of the engine was a sharp reminder. Mandrake shook his head doubtfully. "Possible, but not likely," he said, pointing up at the thick, leafy cover overhead. "If we cannot see the helicopter from the gound, it's quite certain they can't see us from the air. Waste of time. Needle in a haystack."

The sound became more distant, returned, and then died away altogether. After a few minutes' wait, to see whether it would come back again, they renewed their uphill slog.

"What I don't understand is why we haven't seen anything of the Gardiens yet," panted Chip. "If they're as fierce as everyone makes out, why don't they attack us or something?"

"Amen to that, young Chip," grinned King. "I'm just in the mood to be attacked. I've done no fighting these past two days and I'm needing it." Mandrake did not smile. He eased his load and resumed the march.

"To tell the truth," he said a little later. "Be relieved if they did attack us. Greatly relieved." But he offered no explanation for this cryptic remark.

The slope increased sharply and traces of bed rock could be seen through the stony soil. Patches of loose and treacherous shale made progress slow and uncertain. Most of the time they were reduced to crawling, an exhausting and painful business.

They were still following the river, which had carved a deep course through the foothills. Higher up, a series of rapids finally gave way to a torrent, cascading down the rocky gully.

The whole day was spent in working their way obliquely upwards. When they stopped for the night, in the shelter of a great boulder, their hands and knees were cut to ribbons and their clothes to rags. They were too exhausted for food, or for the drop in temperature to stop them sleeping soundly.

Mandrake roused them before dawn to urge them on again so resolutely that by mid-morning, the third of their journey, they reached the plateau from which the walls of the mountains rose sheer and forbidding. They were just below the timber line where all vegetation ceased. The temperature was now so low that, in spite of the exertions of climbing, Chip's teeth were chattering. The others were in no better shape, although Mandrake seemed more determined than ever.

"I trust we have to go no higher, Dr. Mandrake," shivered Mr. Gopal, whose bronze skin had turned to an unhealthy mauve.

"We're doing well," announced Mandrake briskly. "I have no doubt at all that we shall find the Gardiens' sacred city at this level." But it was not until midday that King, who was on ahead, raised a shout. He had reached the edge of a precipitous canyon. His words were lost in the roar of falling water, but as the others joined him, they saw, through the mist thrown up by the waterfall, a great lake, and on the farther side, about two miles away, a group of stone buildings. The smoke from cooking fires hung low over the water.

"That's it," declared Mandrake. "Was quite certain of it all along." Encouraged, they increased their pace. King forged so far ahead that Mandrake called out for him to wait.

"We must approach carefully," he warned. "We still have no idea how they will receive us."

A few minutes later they were glad enough of this caution, for King dropped suddenly to his knees behind a clump of long grass, and waved for the others to do the same.

"Too late," he growled. "The black trousers have beaten us to it. You were right, young Chip." He swept the grass aside and pointed. Floating on the lake beyond the buildings which had previously hidden it from their sight, was the unmistakable shape of a helicopter. King let the grass spring back into place. "Yes, sir," he said. "Black trousers, a pound to a penny."

Mandrake flushed angrily. "They shall not beat us," he said, thrusting his beard out as though it were an offensive weapon. "This is something too big, too dangerous for them to have. We must get away to the other side of the lake, and we must not be seen. This time our lives depend on it."

In spite of their fatigue, the others were impressed enough by his grim expression to follow silently and watchfully as he retraced the route to the falls.

When they had reached the cover of the woods on the opposite shore, Mandrake called a halt. He held up Professor Schumann's leaden casket and looked at them solemnly.

"Quite determined," he said, "not to leave here without a sample of the material that killed that porter. No time for explanations now, but I will tell you this. Unless we can do this and beat the Syndicate in doing so, it will be a disaster not only for the island, but for the whole world." For a moment Chip wondered if the strain had driven Mandrake out of his mind, but one look at the doctor's face satisfied him. Dishevelled and strained though he might be, he certainly was sane and in deadly earnest. "At this moment," went on Mandrake, "someone from the Syndicate is with the Gardiens, trying to find out what Julius Schumann knew. Not succeeded yet, otherwise he would be on his way back to S. Jean. He doesn't know what he is looking for. I do. That is our advantage."

"Yes, but we still don't know where the Flashing Mountain is," said Chip wearily.

"This city was placed here with the express purpose of guarding the mountain. Can't be far off. Must be a track leading to it. Certain of it. If we follow the shore round, we shall find it, and that we must do now. Come!"

He set off impatiently through the trees as though recharged with energy. King swung his sack of explosives over his shoulder, and took Mr. Gopal's pack as well.

"If we can get away from here and go home when Dr. Mandrake gets what he wants," he shivered, "let's go."

The woods seemed cold and still. For the first time since they had started out there was no sound of birds, only an all-enveloping and forbidding silence.

A quarter of a mile farther on, as Mandrake had forecast, they came to a broad track beaten through the trees and running sharply downwards from the direction of the city. At intervals it was marked by blocks of carved stone, which had been eroded by time and weather. Mandrake darted along examining them eagerly.

"This is a processional way," he said triumphantly. "These stones have all the signs of being religious symbols."

He hastened off downhill, leaving the others to follow. The track curved steadily for nearly a mile, and then turned sharply into the face of the mountain. Running upwards before them was a broad stairway cut in the living rock. At the top, two massive obelisks stood out against the sky like sentries, sixty or seventy feet high. As the slanting rays of the afternoon sun reflected from them, Chip caught his breath.

"Did you see?" he demanded shrilly. "Did you see them, Dr. Mandrake? They're all grey, like the costumes and that porter's face."

CHAPTER TEN

FLASHING MOUNTAIN

THEY STOOD silently, all knowing that beyond lay the sinister secret they had come so far to find. Mandrake broke the spell.

"Will one of you come with me? Just one. We have only two robes and masks. They have obviously been exposed to this force already. I believe the grey material is now inert and will give some protection against the radiation. Certain of it."

It had become plain to Chip that the search for the secret of the Flashing Mountain was a challenge he could not evade. In the shape of Malik, Kreamer, Petit and the Syndicate it represented everything he hated and feared and, in the hungry children and down-trodden natives, everything he was prepared to fight for. He knew that if he turned aside now he would never again be sure of himself.

He forced back the choking sensation in his throat. "I'll come," he said firmly.

"Ah, no. It's no place for young Chip," said King. "I'll be with you, Dr. Mandrake."

"I insist. It is my place," wailed Mr. Gopal. "As the servant and friend of Professor Schumann . . ."

It looked as though a ridiculous wrangle would follow, but Chip settled the matter by unrolling one of the costumes and slipping it over his head, before the others could stop him.

"Very well, Chip," said Mandrake. "I would have gladly gone with any one of you. King and Mr. Gopal be good enough to conceal yourselves until we return. Prevent us being surprised if anyone should come." Still grumbling under his breath, King helped Chip adjust the costume, which appeared to have been made for a giant. The mask came down over his head and rested on his shoulders, completely obscuring his view except for the ground immediately before him.

"You take care, boy," murmured King. "Don't let nothing happen to you. Just one shout and old King will be right there beside you." Chip nodded and shuffled towards the rock steps. He found that by tilting the mask back he could improve his view.

Mandrake was already waiting, looking strangely impressive in the grey robe and mask. He put out his hand to touch Chip's shoulder and they started the long ascent together. The steps were deep, but only two or three inches high, which made their shuffling progress slow and ungainly. Before long the heat in his mask became so great that Chip felt perspiration running down his face. He was only kept going by the sight of Mandrake just ahead. He set his teeth doggedly, determined to keep going. In the end he had to push the mask right back to gulp a few breaths of the ice-cold air. Then he saw the obelisks immediately above him.

He flung himself down on the stone platform at the top, and crept breathlessly towards Mandrake, who was already peering over the farther edge.

They were on the lip of an immense crater. Ragged ash-grey sides plunged to a floor thick with grey dust and criss-crossed with deep fissures. The farther side was a towering wall of rock, which formed the eastern end of the basin containing the great lake of the Gardiens.

What seized Chip's attention immediately was the monstrous mass, projecting up through the floor of the crater. A black pillar, contorted and twisted into a nightmare shape, which reared several hundred feet into the air, so that the pinnacle was on a level with the platform on which they lay. From top to bottom it was pitted with cracks and blemishes, as though it had been thrown up molten from the depths and had congealed in an instant. It had such a weird appearance that it might have been part of the landscape of another planet.

Chip shuddered. He felt that he was in the presence of an alien and malignant force from the secret places of the earth.

He did not need telling that this, at last, was the Flashing Mountain, the abode of Xarpata, and the secret of Professor Schumann. He just knew.

Evidently it affected Mandrake similarly, for when he spoke, his voice, muffled by the mask, was shaking.

"Going down into the crater to get a sample of that material. Stay here. Shall signal if I need you."

He lowered himself clumsily over the edge of the platform. When he released his hold, it at once became apparent that the steeply sloping surface was treacherous and unstable. He disappeared in a cloud of grey dust, sliding for fifty or sixty feet before he could regain control. He continued his unsteady descent, losing his footing at every other step, until, two-thirds of the way down, he was finally overtaken by a minor avalanche and carried bodily to the bottom, where he lay motionless and half buried.

Just as Chip had made up his mind to follow, Mandrake staggered up and stood swaying at the edge of a crevasse, his hands over the front of his mask. Chip's desperate shout warned him of his danger, but he was still dazed and having difficulty in seeing properly. Chip hesitated no longer.

Swinging himself over the edge, he glissaded down the loose slope, until, half-blinded, he landed fifty feet or so from where Mandrake was stumbling aimlessly to and fro. He waded through the knee-deep dust to Mandrake.

"Are you all right?" he shouted.

Mandrake made an angry gesture.

". . . should not have come . . . do as I say," he croaked thickly. "Twisted my leg. Nothing, nothing at all. Lost the lead container . . . Must have it."

Chip eased back his mask cautiously. The casket was still hanging by its strap over Mandrake's shoulder. Mandrake coughed explosively when Chip told him.

"Since you're here . . . lean on you," he said gruffly. "Help me over to the centre. I want a sample from deep in one of the cracks below this insulating dust."

Chip half-led, half-dragged him forward. They negotiated the fissures with difficulty, producing clouds of dust at each faltering step. It was a grim, silent struggle, with every sound, except their own laboured breathing, blanketed by the heavy silence.

"Just another few steps, boy," urged Mandrake. "Then leave it to me." Chip braced his shoulders to take the strain again, and counted the steps to himself.

". . . ten . . . eleven . . . twelve."

"That's it," grunted Mandrake. "That will do."

He staggered a few feet up the foot of the misshapen Flashing Mountain to a grey-rimmed cavity, while Chip sank exhausted to his knees and remained like that for several minutes, regaining his breath. Then he was startled by a report like a rifle shot from high up on the rock wall on the farther side.

He tilted his head back and saw a detached boulder followed by a shower of stones bouncing down the near-vertical face. The fall was too far off to create any danger and buried itself harmlessly in the dust. He guessed that it had been loosened by the earth tremors during the last few days. He pushed from his mind the thought of the great mass of water the wall was holding back. He knew that if the rock barrier collapsed, the lake of the Gardiens would discharge directly into the crater and crush them like flies under thousands of tons of water.

As he watched the falling boulder, a movement low on the rock face caught his attention. He glanced towards it and his blood ran cold, for clambering slowly down were three men. From their light colour and great stature, they were easily recognisable as Gardiens. They were naked to the waist, and carried bronze shields and spears which gleamed dully in the sun. Their movements were slow and clumsy, as though weights were attached to their limbs, but their progress was relentless and their intention plain. They had come to kill the intruders who were defiling the home of their god. In their anger they were coming, careless of their own safety, without protective cloaks and masks.

Before he could attract Mandrake's attention, a whole series of reports broke out on the rock face and a large section came plummeting down. Then, with a sound like thunder, the ground beneath their feet began trembling.

Instantly, dust flew up in a whirling cloud, obscuring the sun and plunging the crater into darkness. The earth heaved and groaned convulsively as though in torment.

Chip flung himself flat, covering his head with his arms. Above the roar of the earthquake came sharp, tearing, crackling sounds that pierced his head until he cried out with pain.

As suddenly as it had begun the tremor was over, leaving behind a silence which came down like a curtain. Chip lay dazed, too scared to move. The first thing he became aware of, was an overpowering, sweet smell, like that of decaying fruit, hanging heavily in the air. Mandrake's muffled voice shouted to him from nearby, but he could not understand. Gradually the dust settled, but they had to wait for it to clear completely before it was safe to move over the great cracks yawning in the floor.

Chip glanced up at the Flashing Mountain. It was still intact but appeared to have changed its shape. He stared fascinated at the grey streaks that had appeared like wounds in its grotesque surface, until he realised that Mandrake was again shouting to him. His ears still hurt so much that he could hardly hear.

". . . where are they? . . . disappeared . . ." repeated Mandrake.

Only then did Chip remember the three Gardiens. There was no sign of them on the rock face. They had apparently vanished. Mandrake shook his arm and pointed. Chip caught his breath. For there, behind where the Gardiens had been, were their unmistakable shadows printed on the exposed face. At the foot of each shadow was a pile of grey dust. After a moment's hesitation Mandrake struggled over for a closer examination.

"Let us go from this place as quickly as we can," he said in a hushed voice. "Give me your arm, boy."

Chip was trembling so violently, that thrusting his way back up the dust slopes became almost impossible. Only his determination not to let Mandrake down forced him on. It was like climbing a greasy pole, two steps forward and one back, with no firm foothold to be found. Mandrake became almost a dead weight and several times before reaching the top Chip almost gave up. But finally they lay gasping for breath on the upper rim of the crater.

"No time . . . to hang around," said Mandrake. "Got . . . to get . . . away, boy."

Chip nodded silently and gave a final fearful glance back at the Flashing Mountain. It squatted in its hole like a poisonous serpent, waiting for fresh victims upon which to release its unnatural powers. He shuddered and turned away to the steps. He was aware of a great shadow rising behind him. There was a blinding flash and he felt himself falling into darkness.

CHAPTER ELEVEN

THE END OF XARPATA

When Chip came to his senses it was already dark. He found Mr. Gopal bending over him. He felt, rather than saw, that they were in an enclosed space.

"Do not move, Mr. Wood. You have been struck forcibly on the head," whispered Mr. Gopal. "I think you are not very well."

Ignoring this well-meant advice, Chip raised himself on one elbow. "Where are we?" he asked, wincing at the pain in his head. "What's happened?"

"Ay, we have been captured by the Gardiens. All of us. We are in the city by the lake. This is most unfortunate, you will agree."

"Sneaked up behind us," rumbled the voice of King bitterly. "Never so much as smelt them. Blindfolded us and brought us here."

"Dr. Mandrake," called Chip anxiously. "Is . . ."

"Yes, I'm here, boy. Leg's done up though. Twice its usual size. But, are you all right now? Worried the life out of me."

"I think so, but what's going to happen to us?"

"Don't know. No one has spoken to us since we've been here. Treated us as though we had the plague. Put all our belongings in here with us. Taken nothing. Strange people. Been chanting half the night, only just stopped."

King's voice came again, farther away.

"These walls are solid stone all round," he growled disgustedly.

"I've still got my sack, Dr. Mandrake. Do you think I could try a stick of dynamite, say? Blow a hole in the wall?"

"And in us too," snapped Mandrake. "Don't be a fool. Chip, come over here, closer to me."

Chip groped his way towards Mandrake's voice.

"Listen carefully, boy. Greatest importance. Must get this lead casket back to Richard Liberté in S. Jean. You will escape and take it. He must help you smuggle it off the island, to a friend of mine, Dr. Bowen, at the United Nations in New York. Absolutely vital."

Chip blinked, wondering if Mandrake's injury was making him delirious. Escape—S. Jean—United Nations—New York, and they were shut in a stone cell, in the mountains of the Gardiens. Mandrake must have sensed Chip's hesitation, for he went on with greater emphasis.

"Most devilish discovery in the history of man, Chip. Must not fall into the hands of people like Malik. Greatest source of radioactive power ever discovered. Convinced of it. No costly processes, no elaborate plant. Just lying there waiting to be used. Scattered from bombers, could wipe out whole nations—poison whole continents. No explosion, just a fine powder of the raw material. It can never be of use to humanity. Never!"

"But . . . " began Chip helplessly.

"Don't believe me? Look at the Gardiens. Used to cover the island, now there's just a handful of them. Biggest mistake of their lives to move up here. Being slowly killed off, just being near it. All these earth tremors breaking up natural insulation and releasing more radioactivity. They're all sick, going blind, wasting away, going deaf. Form of radiation sickness. Convinced of it."

"But how *can* I escape?" burst out Chip.

"Thought of that. As I see it, only one chance. King

and Mr. Gopal be good enough to listen. When that door is opened, you, King, will throw a piece of dynamite through it. Be ready with a second piece. In the confusion, Chip, you will try to get away. Is that clear?"

They were silent for a while.

"I know it's a forlorn hope," continued Mandrake more soberly. "Must be tried. It's our duty to try."

Chip rubbed his aching head tenderly. Although he was finding it difficult to think clearly, he saw that Mandrake's scheme was doomed to failure before it started. Supposing he were able to break away, which seemed unlikely enough, what chance would he have of reaching S. Jean with all the Gardiens after him? He thought of the helicopter lying on the lake and wondered whether it offered any hope, but none of them could fly it. In any case it was probably guarded. It was plain that if he got away, it would have to be on foot.

"I'll have a shot at it," he agreed reluctantly. "I'll do my best, Dr. Mandrake."

"Good boy. Rest of us will hinder any pursuit. King, get over by the door and be ready."

They sat in silence for a long time, too disheartened to talk. The chanting started again, a deep rhythmic murmur, reminding Chip of the rise and fall of the sea.

"Must be four-five hundred of them Gardiens fellers out there," said King. "Going to need a lot of that dynamite to shift them."

"Fear you're right," agreed Mandrake bitterly. "Pity that rock wall didn't collapse during the earthquake. Would have flooded the crater. Saved us a lot of trouble."

Chip thought about that, picturing what would have happened to Mandrake and himself if the wall had been breached. The Flashing Mountain might have been drowned, they certainly would have been. Still, there was the seed of an idea there. He wished his head would stop throbbing so that he could think more clearly, but before he could arrive at any conclusion, King sprang to his feet.

"They're coming. I can hear them. Better get ready."

Chip crept up behind him, nervously clutching the lead casket.

Footsteps halted outside. The door was flung open, admitting a flood of grey light and a view over the great lake. King launched himself forward, his arm swinging in a great arc. A few seconds later, an explosion reverberated from the surface of the water far below. Then a familiar voice from outside said:

"That was unwise, Dr. Mandrake. I have come to help you," and Jason Kreamer stepped in through the doorway, his pale eyes showing up like a cat's in the darkness. Petit crept in after him, followed by two Gardiens carrying flaming torches. The fiery light gleamed on the automatic in Kreamer's hand.

"A wild attempt," he said, glancing contemptuously at King. "There's only a narrow ledge outside, and a long drop to the lake, so you could not succeed in dynamiting your way out, if that was your intention. It was foolish of our friends to leave dangerous explosives in your hands, but they are superstitious people and think everything you possess is unclean." He looked round for Mandrake. "In fact, Dr. Mandrake, they think you, yourselves, are unclean. That is unfortunate because I understand you have penetrated into one of their holy places. Most unwise."

"Well, that settles the matter, Kreamer, doesn't it?" Mandrake's beard jutted pugnaciously above hectically flushed cheeks. "We're in their hands, aren't we?"

Kreamer ignored the interruption.

"That alone would have been enough for them to kill you, but what has finally decided them you must die, was learning that you were responsible for the death of Professor Schumann. Apparently, they had great faith and trust in him. Perhaps I should not have told them. They were most angry. Josef Malik thought they would be. He is a most shrewd man."

Goaded beyond bearing by Kreamer's sardonic manner, Mandrake bellowed furiously and hurled a boot at him. It missed and struck Petit a glancing blow on the face. The small man leapt forward, his knife ready, but Kreamer restrained him and went on evenly:

"Believe me, I have no wish for you to be killed. In fact, Malik has sent me in his private helicopter to search for you, in case you were in danger. I can get you away by air, if you choose, but you must do so quickly. The Gardiens have given me only a short time to talk to you. Then they are coming. My interpreter tells me that they are going to give you to their god. It sounds nonsense, but is no doubt unpleasant."

"Kreamer, no time for double talk," burst out Mandrake. "You'll get no help from me. If you want Schumann's discovery, find it for yourself. Obviously the Gardiens have not told you, otherwise you wouldn't be here now. Get out! Leave us alone!"

"Let me work on the boy," snarled Petit. "That will make the old goat talk."

Kreamer thought for a moment then shrugged his shoulders.

"Very well, Louis. It will be quicker, perhaps."

Petit grinned in anticipation and came stealthily across the cell. King gathered himself, but the blunt nose of Kreamer's automatic swung round menacingly. Chip backed away until he was against the wall and could go no farther. Petit came after him slowly, his narrow eyes glittering in his twitching face. His breath hissed between clenched teeth, bared in a cat-like grin. His knife flickered in the guttering torchlight as though it had a life of its own.

"Stop," roared Kreamer. "What is in that container the boy's carrying?"

But Petit seemed to be in a world of his own, for he paid no attention, creeping steadily after Chip. Kreamer took two strides and felled him with a blow across the neck.

"Get the container," he said. "Get it!"

Petit obeyed, his eyes blinking, as though he had just awoken from a deep sleep.

"Don't open it, Kreamer," snapped Mandrake. "Don't let him open it."

Kreamer smiled slowly. "Open it, Louis," he said triumphantly, "over by the light."

Petit took the casket under the torches and tugged at the catch.

"Hide your faces!" shouted Mandrake.

Chip covered his head with his robe and ducked.

The cell was filled with a crackling sound like a high-voltage discharge, and a second later, by a piercing scream.

When Chip looked up, the door was open and the casket gone. Petit was teetering on the rock ledge outside, his hands clawing at his face. With another long-drawn-out cry, he arched over backwards and disappeared, falling to the lake far below. Chip shrank back, for as Petit fell, his hands had come away from his face, revealing a repulsive grey mask. As in the crater, a sickly smell of rotting fruit hung heavily in the air.

There was complete silence in the hut for a moment, broken only by the moaning of the two Gardiens, who lay flat on their faces. Kreamer crouched against the wall, aghast at what he had seen.

"Is that . . . ?" he mouthed. "Where did you . . . ?"

Chip stared back at him blankly. His mind suddenly

cleared, so that his thoughts came straight again. With the casket gone, escape was useless. It was only a matter of time before Kreamer discovered the crater. Now that he had some idea of what the secret was, he would be keener on the scent than ever, and then, in spite of anything they could do, the Flashing Mountain would be in his hands. The President would persuade himself that it was in the interests of the island to grant further concessions to Malik's Syndicate, who would then be free to exploit the deadly mineral and sell it to the highest bidder, to anyone, if the price was right. Silverman's motto came back like a slap in the face. "Anything if the price is right, boy."

Chip forgot about his throbbing head and about being scared of the Gardiens and Kreamer. He forgot his fear of choking and of everything else, and started feeling angry instead. Angry for Julius Schumann, for Mr. Gopal, Richard Liberté, and all the natives on the island. Angry at the Silvermans, the Maliks, the Kreamers, the Syndicate . . .

He lashed out wildly at Kreamer, who was staggering to his feet. Then he grabbed the sack of explosives and Mandrake's protective robe, and, shouting to King, darted out on to the rock ledge.

All the Gardiens, several hundred of them, had gathered at the edge of the lake where Petit had fallen, their prisoners forgotten for the moment.

Taking advantage of the distraction, he raced along the high ground, towards the end of the lake where the crater lay. Mandrake's words were echoing through his head, ". . . pity that rock wall didn't collapse . . . pity that rock wall didn't collapse . . ." Well, it would collapse, and he would see that it did. He would see that Malik and the Syndicate did not get their hands on the Flashing Mountain.

"Put this on, King," he yelled, flinging over Mandrake's

costume. "Come down after me." He ran to the edge of the rock wall, where the dust began, and flung himself down the slope. King landed a few feet away and picked up the sack.

"You're a mad fool, son. You could've blown us to kingdom come. What are we doing this for, anyhow."

"Dynamite the base of the wall. Bring it down and empty the lake into the crater. We've got to, King, please."

King eyed the wall and stared up fearfully at the Flashing Mountain.

"You sure are mad, young Chip," he muttered. "I don't know whether there is enough dynamite to do it, or enough fuse for us to get out of here before it blows up. I sure as anything don't want to be down here when it does."

Still grumbling to himself and shooting anxious glances around the crater, King laid out about a dozen sticks of dynamite and a case of detonators, and then unwound a coil of fuse. Together, they strung out the fuse, placing the dynamite and detonators in a crack in the centre of the wall.

"Ain't had much experience," said King. "Don't know how fast this burns." He held a match to the tip of the fuse. "How do we get out?"

"Up the rock face," said Chip tersely.

"Over this lot? If it blows while we're up there, I'll be seeing you at the pearly gates. Least I hope I will. You sure you mean this?"

Chip nodded briefly. The fuse spluttered into life.

"Out, boy. Fast as you can," grunted King.

They went up the rock face as though the fuses were fixed to their own tails. What must have taken Chip and Mandrake more than three-quarters of an hour, now took only minutes. King worked like a dynamo, heaving Chip up ahead in long, powerful movements. Their grey robes, ripped to ribbons by the sharp surface, were streaked with blood.

Chip expected at any moment to hear the first rumble of the explosion, which would bring the rocks about their ears and send them crashing back into the crater.

"Now, get away from here, boy," shouted King hoarsely, shoving Chip over the rim. "Run!"

But Chip was too exhausted even to get to his feet. King levered himself over the top, slung Chip across his shoulder, and staggered drunkenly away from the lake.

Before he had taken ten paces, the ground heaved as the charges detonated. Blindly he flung himself onward. The base of the wall blew out, leaving an arch of rock poised above the void, as the waters of the lake began to move. King threw Chip to the farther side and leaped wildly as the ground buckled beneath him. Chip rolled over on the grass as King thudded down beside him.

Speechless, they looked back at the unfolding spectacle. The bed of the lake had been fractured so that water was sluicing through into the crater. As the flow increased, the rocks splintered and the entire wall moved with deafening creaks and groans.

King pointed. Chip saw the helicopter taxi-ing on the lake, making a desperate effort to take off. Revolving slowly, it drifted with the undertow of the outfall towards the crater, then, with a burst of power, it lurched into the air, as the wall finally gave way. For a moment it staggered in the turbulence, before the down-draught caused by the moving mass of water seized it like an invisible hand, dragging it downward.

A bulky figure, which Chip instantly recognised as Kreamer, leapt out. Turning over and over, the German fell with unbelievable slowness, to vanish into the mælstrom beneath. The helicopter immediately went out of control, plunging vertically, until it was shattered against the crest of the Flashing Mountain.

With the collapse of the wall, the liberated waters of the lake surged forward.

"The Mountain," screamed Chip. "The Flashing Mountain, it's moving."

The great pillar appeared to stagger under the impact of the water. White fingers of foam leapt up its black and twisted surface, as though straining to tear it down. Slowly, almost imperceptibly at first, but with gathering speed, it moved downwards, sending shock waves shuddering through the ground, which brought avalanches thundering into the crater. The violence of the tremors increased, until Chip thought he and King would be swept away. Then, with a final convulsion the Flashing Mountain was gone, buried beneath the rising flood.

A cold, white light blazed for an instant, far below the surface, then it too vanished, leaving nothing but the seething waters. The eyes of Xarpata had closed for ever.

The harbour of S. Jean was empty except for a few fishing craft. The *Midas* had gone, carrying Josef Malik in search of greater profits at less risk in some other quarter of the globe. Obviously he had crossed the Island of the Four Apostles off his list, for he had abandoned the black-uniformed men who had been fighting his battle ashore, and ordered the *Midas* to slip silently from her anchorage under cover of darkness. During the southward trek of Mandrake and his party to the land of the Gardiens, Malik had attempted to take over the island by force and if Richard Liberté had not thrown his men into the bitter street fighting on the side of the President's troops there was no doubt the attempt would have succeeded. As it was, when the news of the destruction of the Flashing Mountain had reached the capital, Malik had taken his departure and the sign of the mailed fist had disappeared from the harbour. It had disappeared from S. Jean as well, for disheartened by Malik's flight, the black-uniformed forces had caved in and surrendered.

Chip smiled faintly, although truth to tell he was not feeling much like smiling at all, as he heard King and Mr. Gopal starting to quarrel somewhere in the garden below. They had been bickering ever since the escape from the mountains. It was difficult to believe they were such firm friends, but they were, in spite of Mr. Gopal's persistent efforts to convince King of the wickedness of violence.

King's deep laugh rang out across the garden, awakening Mandrake, who started up in his chair and clutched the small wooden box he had been carrying all day. He had been making a mystery of the box ever since he had received it from America the previous night. He had been happy enough, during the last three weeks, pottering around the President's garden, while Chip had fretted against the enforced inactivity. Since his experience in the great crater Chip had lost his nervousness, and in fact, felt that he would never again be deeply afraid of anything. He had wanted to be with Richard Liberté, who had been directing the fight against the Syndicate forces at the docks, but this, Mandrake had refused to allow. Now, it was all over anyhow, and Chip was feeling disgruntled, most of all at the prospect of returning with Mandrake to England. They were due to sail in a few days and were, in fact, waiting to take their leave of the President. Chip thought gloomily of exchanging the sun and his new-found friends for London, the docks, and yes, there was always Silverman to look forward to, as well. He was not worried about Silverman, but all the same was not looking forward to their next encounter.

He became aware that Mandrake was eyeing him closely and was about to ask why, when the doors of the President's office were thrown open. The President and Richard Liberté came out on to the terrace.

Chip stared rather enviously at Liberté, who seemed to have gained self-confidence, as though the success of his fight against the Syndicate had proved something for him. The President also had changed. For several days his life had been threatened by Malik's black-uniformed men and only Richard's intervention had saved him. He looked resigned and relaxed, no longer worried by the events which had overtaken him. He rested his hand on Liberté's shoulder and smiled rather ironically at Mandrake.

"You see, Dr. Mandrake. The Syndicate have gone and the so-called Revolutionary Freedom Party has come to take their place. Permit me to introduce my new deputy, my son Richard."

Chip and Mandrake stared at Richard Liberté as though they had never seen him before.

"Your *son!*" exclaimed Mandrake. "Preposterous! Bless my soul!"

"As you say," agreed the President wryly. "Preposterous; but it is so. You are the first to hear of it."

Chip stared from one to the other, remembering how he had thought on first seeing Liberté that there was a resemblance to the President. Now, as they stood side by side it was quite marked. He remembered, too, how King had said that Liberté had stopped his followers from trying to shoot the President.

"But why . . .?" he burst out, only half convinced, then flushed, realising he was talking out of turn.

"Why?" echoed the President, good-humouredly. "That is a long story. I sent Richard and his mother to France soon after he was born. She did not support this hot climate well. Also, I wanted my son to have a French education. This, as you see, he has had. He has learned of the wickedness of presidents and the art of revolution— a full education."

"That's not fair," protested Liberté.

"You mean you have not seen him since then?" demanded Mandrake, incredulously. "That the Syndicate knew nothing of this?"

"You do not believe me, Dr. Mandrake? Yes, of course, I saw my wife and son when I visited France, usually once a year. It was not much, but when the Syndicate showed their true colours I did not want my family here—to become hostages. However, Richard was impatient. He returned without a word to anyone, two years ago, using a forged passport and a false name. I tell you, Dr. Mandrake, you professors do not know what young people learn to do in universities. The Syndicate believed that my son was still in France and that 'Richard Liberté' was just another young trouble-maker, with his revolutionary party. The price of education, Dr. Mandrake! I only discovered all this because I am not as inefficient as he thinks. I took great pains to keep his secret, for the sake of us both."

"It was all against the Syndicate," rapped Liberté, annoyed by his father's bantering tone. "I wanted to expel them and hold elections."

"I know that. Malik knew it too. It was difficult to protect you from him; he wanted me to have you shot. However, that is all beside the point now. You—and your young friend Charles Wood here, have, between you, expelled the Syndicate. The price I must pay, Dr. Mandrake, for the revolutionary party's help is to appoint Richard my deputy and hold elections in twelve months' time. Due to the stupidity and ignorance of the population, he will undoubtedly win and I shall then be thrown out."

"You have agreed to this?" asked Mandrake.

The President's good humour disappeared briefly. He nodded:

"I shall be glad to go. It is not pleasant to be hated year after year. But," he glanced in a half-amused way at Liberté, "I will help you to organise the island to starve peacefully before I go. You will not find it easy without the Syndicate, much as you hated them."

"The natives will have freedom," proclaimed Liberté proudly. "We shall work together to create a new prosperity, even if it means hardships at first."

"I hope they will be grateful," replied his father. "Who will help you? Young Charles Wood, perhaps."

"Yes, I will," blurted out Chip, before realising that the President had been laughing at Liberté. Then he flushed again uncomfortably, but added defiantly: "King and Mr. Gopal said they wanted to stay too."

"You'll be welcome, Chip," said Liberté. "You stay. I'll need every bit of help I can get."

Mandrake straightened his injured leg and stood up carefully. "Seems to settle that," he said. "If you really want to, Chip, I'll try to get permission from your aunt for you to stay. Returning to England myself. No longer have any heart for excavating the Gardiens' city. But I, too, can make a contribution before I go. Here"—he tossed the small wooden box he had brought with him to Liberté— "Open that. It will at least prevent starvation here."

Liberté prised back the lid and looked up at Mandrake puzzled.

"It is just a lump of rock," he exclaimed. "Is this a joke?"

"No joke," said Mandrake. "Far from it. That means food, new machinery, and probably the smelting plant you need."

The President picked up the piece of grey and white stone curiously: "And this is, Dr. Mandrake?"

"Silver, your excellency, silver. It is the white wife of the god Xarpata. All know the legend of the brown and white wives buried in the island. Brown wife stood for copper—white wife for silver. Always mean something, these legends. Never fail."

"But where?" demanded the President. "The Syndicate geologists searched the whole island north of the Copper Belt. South of there, in the forests or the mountains, we should never raise the money to work it—unless we called in another Syndicate."

"No, not another . . . " shouted Liberté.

Mandrake held up his hand.

"Didn't search here." He tapped his stick on the ground. "Under your palace. That's where the white wife is, in the hill of S. Jean."

"How did you discover this?" asked the President. "And when?"

"First day here. Saw this piece of quartz, studded with the stuff. Then the inscriptions to *La Dame Blanche* set me thinking. Believe the first governor, your ancestor, knew about the silver. Probably afraid to work it in case the French Government took the island from him, so he left the inscription as a hint. May be wrong, of course, but think not."

"Are you sure this is really silver, Dr. Mandrake?" demanded Liberté.

Mandrake nodded.

"Directly the Syndicate gave up I sent a sample to my friend Bowen in New York. Had it analysed. Had the reply yesterday. Rich deposit. Native silver. Just waiting to be taken from the ground. No shafts; work it from the surface." He shook his finger under Liberté's nose.

"Won't solve your problems, you know. Ignorance, stupidity, and just plain greed will be your problems. This will keep you from starving while you think about them, that's all."

There was silence for a moment before Liberté, struck by the idea, said: "This means the fort and palace will have to be demolished. The symbols of privilege and tyranny will have to be destroyed for the welfare of the people."

They all stared at him. Then the President started laughing. The sound rang out across the terrace, so that the secretary, Vincent, came to see what was the matter with him, but he paid no attention and went on laughing, as though he had seen the joke of a lifetime and would never stop.

THE END